# BILLIONAIRE RETREAT

BILLIONAIRE MATCHMAKER
BOOK FOUR

SUMMER COOPER

LOVY BOOKS

Lovy Books Ltd
20-22 Wenlock Road
London N1 7GU

Cover by SC Creative

# PART 1

**Falling and Failing**

I shouldn't have worn a thong. I always went overboard and now my exposed butt cheeks were paying the price, I thought to myself, as I attempted not to show how uncomfortable I was sitting on the hot ground waiting for my number to be called.

I looked at the other girls around me who were also scantily clad, but at least they had some clothes on, which was more than could be said for me. To be honest, a lot of women in L.A. walked around in bikinis, so I didn't feel too out of place. But my thong-bikini swimsuit covered in sequins was probably too much even for Los Angeles. I looked like a desperate Vegas showgirl.

As I shifted uncomfortably, I looked over the crowd in front of me. We were all nervously waiting for our big break, but I refused to do it standing up. We were going to be here for hours whether I stood in line or not. I wanted to break Kenny in half for the mess he had gotten me into. Firstly, this swimsuit had been his idea. Secondly, I didn't appreciate sitting on a curb outside of an abandoned building, half-naked, hoping I was in the right place. When I got home, I promised myself I would wring Kenny's neck.

Kenny was my little cousin, agent and landlord. He taught kickboxing and cycling at a boutique gym for the ultra-wealthy when he wasn't moonlighting as my agent. In truth, I hadn't asked him to be my agent; he signed himself up for the role. And as I expected, he wasn't much good at it.

I had only moved to L.A. two weeks ago and Kenny, being the doting cousin that he was, had decided to take me under his wing. He wanted to show me the ropes. Kenny knew nothing about Hollywood or acting, but he assumed living in L.A. made him qualified by default.

Against my better judgment, when he told me about the casting call for swimsuit models for a random reality TV show and suggested I wear something racy to get myself noticed, I decided that maybe he was right. So I decided to wear this horrific swimsuit. Kenny and his boyfriend, Cyril, had done a good job convincing me that it was a good idea.

"Flaunt your assets," Cyril had said. I was flaunting my assets alright, most of my ass was on show.

At one point, I noticed two different lines seemed to be forming, so I eventually I stood up and made my way to the shorter one, hoping that I wouldn't have to waste an entire day auditioning for a role where I just stood around wearing a bikini and smiling into a camera.

Hours later, I finally made it into a nondescript room that contained a desk and a few chairs. Sitting behind the desk was a scowling elderly woman and a younger man who wore an easy smile as if life amused him. Or maybe my swimsuit amused him.

"Where are your clothes?" were the first words out of the woman's mouth.

"I thought this was a… umm… swimsuit model audition…" I said, feeling my cheeks heat. The guy looked embarrassed for me.

"Clearly not." The old lady's tone was curt and made me feel even more foolish. Her distaste towards me was almost palpable. She fingered the pearls around her neck and shook her head disapprovingly as she studied me.

"I think the swimsuit model auditions were across the hall. They finished up an hour ago," the guy volunteered kindly.

"I must have been confused. There were two lines and I had assumed the shorter line was for… never mind… Anyway, sorry for wasting your time." I awkwardly stood there, trying to plan a graceful exit. I knew that as soon as I turned around, they would know more about my body than my ex-boyfriend. I side-shuffled towards the door with as much dignity as I could muster.

"You should be sorry. We're busy people," said the old woman bitterly as she watched me shuffle away. I was astounded by her level of rudeness.

Being a big softie, I immediately wanted to cry. I could feel my voice thickening as I said, "Don't worry, I have no intention of further wasting your time." I gave up saving my pride and just turned to leave. As expected, the old lady gasped once she saw my almost bare butt and I felt myself turning beet red. I wondered if my butt turned red too.

I tried to think of something to say, maybe a really good exit line, so that she would feel terrible for treating me so badly. All I could come up with was, "Thank you for your time."

I wanted to tell her that I didn't need to put up with her condescending attitude, but I was always polite, even when it was undeserved. In fact, being polite was probably my biggest flaw. I was one of those people who apologized to inanimate objects if I bumped into them.

"Miss… what did you say your name was?" called the guy. I turned my face in his direction even though I kept my hand on the door handle.

"Nina. Nina Charles."

"Well, Ms. Charles, you came all this way for an interview," he said in a friendly tone. "And even if it's for the wrong job, you might as well stick around."

"Richard!" the old woman hissed, but Richard ignored her.

He had a point. "What's the job?" I asked, letting go of the handle and turning to face him fully. I kept my gaze directed at the guy, trying to ignore the fact that the old lady was glowering at him.

"We have an island property off the coast of Mexico. Part of it has been converted into a resort. It's not like your typical resort, think of it more as a glamorous camp for the wealthy."

"Okay," I said, wondering what he was getting at.

"We're looking for camp counselors, or 'Entertainment Specialists', as we like to call them."

I hated the outdoors, detested the bugs, but I needed a job. And how bad could it be? After all, if it was designed for rich people it had to be pretty amazing. Not to mention, I couldn't live off Kenny's kindness forever. I needed a real income. My acting career would just have to wait.

"So, it's a resort and camp in one?"

"It's more of a glamping experience. It's for well-off individuals. We host a lot of private parties there. That sort of thing."

I nodded as if I knew what glamping was, but I didn't.

"Where are you from, young lady?" asked the older woman suddenly.

"Georgia."

"Atlanta?" she asked hopefully.

"No. I'm from an area called Regions."

"Never heard of it."

"Most people haven't."

"It must be insignificant."

Gosh, she was a piece of work! She made that comment in such a way, it was almost as if she were daring me to tell her differently.

I shrugged off her rudeness, "Maybe to some people it's insignificant, but it's home to me."

The guy smiled so I gave him a tentative smile back.

"So, do you have any talents, Miss… I'm sorry—what's your name again?" asked Richard.

"Nina. Nina Charles."

"That's different. We've met about 10 Kaitlyn's today. Kaitlyn with a Y. Kaitlin with an I. Exhausting," he said with a huge yawn.

"Well, my middle name is Katherine, so it's close to Kaitlyn. But no, no hidden talents."

"Why am I not surprised?" mumbled the woman.

The man shot her an annoyed glance.

The woman ignored him and said with a false, stiff smile, "Well, leave your resume and we'll be in touch."

I grimaced and the guy looked at me with pity in his eyes. "You don't have a resume, do you?"

My shoulders sagged in defeat, but then I perked up when I remembered that I did have my portfolio at least.

With a smile, I walked towards him and he reached for it, but the old lady was quick. She beat him to it as she promptly snatched it out of my hands. "I'll take that." She didn't even look at it. She just tossed it on the table, placed her elbows on it and folded her hands together.

"I think we're done here. Aren't we, Richard?" she asked coldly.

Richard sighed as he pushed his chair back, clearly frustrated with the old woman, and said, "We'll be in touch, Ms. Charles."

"Thank you," I said softly, turning and heading out the door.

I heard the old woman scream, "Next!" as I made my way down the hall.

"Well, that went well," I said to myself as I held back tears. That would have been my first official audition, IF I had actually been in the correct line.

I sighed as I searched for my car. Feeling dejected, I wandered around aimlessly, angry with myself for messing up the audition, getting angrier by the second as I realized I had completely forgotten where I left my car. I was such an airhead. Finally, I spotted it across the parking lot and I took a step off the walkway towards it. As I did, a car came barreling towards me and I screamed as the driver stepped on the brakes, but the car didn't slow down. I continued screaming. My brain told me to get out of the way, but in my terror, my feet were glued in place. And just like that it was over. The car screeched to a halt just an inch from colliding with me.

I placed my hands on my heart and collapsed against a wall. My legs felt like wet noodles and they could barely hold me up. I slid down the wall and placed my head in my hands, trying to breathe.

A few seconds later, a car door slammed shut and I felt warm hands on my shoulder and heard a voice telling me to breathe.

"You're okay. Just breathe. You're okay," a strong masculine voice said, over and over. I felt myself shaking and without thinking, I wrapped my arms around my body, hugging myself. As I did, I looked up at the stranger squatting in front of me, looking down with dark brown eyes full of concern.

"Hi," he said softly. He took my hand and never broke eye contact with me as he helped me stand up.

Once we were fully standing and my legs didn't feel as if they would give out at any minute, I realized he was much taller than I'd expected. He was at least 6'4 and apparently doing very well for himself, I thought, as I studied his three-piece suit that clearly wasn't off the rack. He had short dark brown hair. He didn't have a mustache or beard, which seemed to accentuate just how perfectly masculine his face was. His jawline was strong, his lips full, his nose a little off-centered, as if it had been broken once before. But of course, his most arresting features were his eyes that studied me with much concern.

"Are you okay, miss?" he asked as he let go of my hand. His hand had enveloped mine and the feel of it had been reassuring. I instantly missed his warmth.

I tried to smile, but failed. I brought a shaky hand up to my face and pushed my bangs away from my eyes.

"I'm fine. Just a little shaken up, I guess." I sounded breathless. I felt breathless, but it was hard to tell if that was because I'd almost been run over by a car or if it was because the man in front of me was so freaking sexy.

"This parking lot can be dangerous for pedestrians. I didn't even see you until you were directly in front of us."

"Thank God for your quick reflexes."

He shook his head. "I'm a terrible driver. It was my driver's reflexes that stopped you from being killed."

It was then that I saw the guy standing near the hood of the car staring at me.

"I'm sorry I almost hit you. If it wasn't for Griff saying something, I would have plowed right into you."

I assumed Griff was the big guy still looking at me intently. He looked afraid to leave my side. I guess I seemed fragile to him. I certainly felt fragile at that moment.

I had to laugh at the sucky day I was having. "It's ok, I'm not going to faint," I tried to reassure him.

"You sure?" he asked clearly not believing me.

I smiled. "I'm sure. Thank you, though."

Griff nodded and took a step back, as if emotionally removing himself from the situation.

"We'll be on our way then."

He walked to his Bentley and I watched, still a little afraid to use my legs. I wasn't sure if I'd faint or not after all.

The driver waved at me one last time, "Sorry about that."

I gave him a partial smile. "I survived."

He laughed at my attempt at a joke and I watched him drive away. I couldn't help myself as I looked towards the guy he called Griff. I smiled in his direction and he gave me a little smile back.

When his car was completely gone, I put my hands on my hips and sighed. If I were keeping score, I would say L.A. had five million points and I had none.

I finally found my car and some obnoxious dude honked at me and yelled, "Nice ass, sweetheart!"

I ignored him and swung myself behind the wheel, defeated. It was then that I realized that not once had Griff or his driver ogled me. Probably the only two nice guys left in L.A., I thought bitterly to myself as I focused on getting home.

My phone rang and I reached for it.

"Hello," I said knowing that my cousin Kenny was on the other end.

"So, how'd it go?" he asked excitedly. "Did you get the part? Tell me you got the part!"

I laughed bitterly. "Let's see. Stood in the wrong line for hours. Got insulted by a cranky old lady. Spent half the day with my butt hanging out. And almost got hit by a car. In short, I did not get the part."

"Oh, Nina," he said. "It sounds like your day sucked."

I was ready to agree, but then I remembered the feel of Griff's hands as he helped me up. I remembered the concern on his face and suddenly not everything seemed that bad.

I reassessed my day. "Actually, it wasn't that bad." I paused for emphasis and then added in a sing-song voice, "I met a man."

"You met a man?" he squeaked. "Hold on, I'm putting you on speaker phone. Cyril! Get over here! She met a man!"

"A man!" I heard Cyril gasp, "I'm so jealous!"

"What?" Kenny said, clearly upset.

"She's only been here two weeks! It took me two years to meet someone," moaned Cyril.

"Guys, guys, can we focus on me?"

But they were already talking among themselves, completely forgetting about me on the other end. I hung up, knowing they would call me back. And in the silence of the car, I wondered what the chances would be that I would see Griff again.

2

———

$\mathcal{I}$ was having a racy dream that involved a certain man in a three-piece suit, except in my dream he was stepping out of a pool wearing nothing but a smile, when my phone woke me up abruptly. I felt around for it, knocking it onto the floor.

Opening one eye, I stuck my hand out and searched for it blindly. The ringing stopped but as soon as I had the phone in my hand the ringing began again. Whoever it was, they were persistent.

I answered with a sleepy, "Hey, this is Nina."

"Hi, Nina. Sorry to call so early in the morning, but we have an opening at the resort and I was wondering if you would be interested. Sorry for the short notice, but we had a last-minute cancellation."

"Who is this? I'm sorry… I'm just waking up," I said. I'd gone out drinking with Kenny and Cyril the night before. I was a light weight, I only needed a couple of beers, but I felt as if I had had a whole case by myself.

"I'm sorry. This is Richard. You gave me your portfolio…"

"Oh yeah, the guy with the cranky old lady," I said sleepily and then immediately slapped my hand over my mouth and was suddenly wide awake. I couldn't believe I'd just said that out loud.

But apparently, Richard wasn't in the least bothered. In fact, he laughed at my faux pas.

"Yep. I guess she made quite an impression."

"You can say that again. So, can you tell me more about what you need me to do? Is this for the entertainment specialist position?"

"Yep. The entertainment specialist keeps the guests happy and attends to their needs. Think of it as a glorified hostess meets babysitter, but for adults." I laughed at his description and he continued, "We'll need you for seven days. Would that be a problem? And I assume you have a passport, right?"

I nodded and then realized that he couldn't see me. "Yeah, I have one. Never been used."

"Well, great. Now's the chance. So, I'm going to have my assistant, Gertrude, get in touch with you. She'll go over all the logistics."

"Ok. Great. Before you go, I forgot to ask. How much does it pay? And when would I need to be there?"

"You'll need to leave today, as soon as possible actually. And we pay one thousand a week and, of course, we provide you with free food and lodging while you're on the island. Top of the line accommodation. Every specialist has her own room and an extensive wardrobe, so you don't even need to pack a lot of clothes."

I was speechless for a second. In my hometown, working at the local movie theater, I barely made $1000 a month as the manager.

"Nina, you still there?"

"Yes, so let me get this right... One thousand for a week? And I leave right away?"

He must have taken my hesitation for uncertainty, as he rushed to reassure me saying, "I understand it's short notice, so I can up the rate to fifteen hundred if that works for you?"

"Sure. I mean, that's great. Thanks for that." I was now standing and pacing the floor, super-excited at the prospect of earning $1500 in a week. My luck was clearly turning around.

"Excellent! I think this will be a wonderful opportunity for you. Gertrude will call you in about half an hour."

"Ok... great... great..." I couldn't stop saying "great". I felt like such a dork. "Thanks, Richard. I really appreciate the opportunity."

"No, thank you, Nina. I'm sure you'll be the perfect

companion for our guest." He thanked me again before hanging up.

"Perfect companion?" I said to myself, curious about his last statement. He made it sound as if someone was renting me for the night.

I paused. Oh, God. I hoped I hadn't just signed on to be an escort. I groaned, feeling stupid. But then I thought to myself, surely that old woman with pretentious sensibilities wouldn't be interviewing people for an escort position. Unless she was some sort of pimp. I giggled at the thought and made a note to ask Gertrude for more details when she called.

Six hours later, I found myself sitting with a group of five other women. We were all chatting excitedly. Well, I wasn't chatting, but I was excited even though no one was actually talking to me. I noticed that I was the only girl with dark hair in the group. Everyone else had long blonde hair and light-colored eyes. There were a few dirty blondes, but I was the only one with straight jet-black hair, dark brown eyes and slightly tanned skin. My mother was Turkish and my biological dad was Colombian, at least that's what my mom told me. She hadn't been too sure since she had only talked to him for a few hours in a bar before conceiving me in the back of his car, a story only made known to me after my Aunt Akila got drunk one night and blurted it out at a family get together when I was about twelve.

My mother had been furious, and Aunt Akila wasn't invited to another family gathering ever again. I hadn't known my high-achieving mother had such a colored past. After all, Mom was a pillar of the community, having become a well-respected doctor in our hometown. She had met and married David Charles, a nice business consultant from Atlanta who was a sarcastic, no-nonsense type, but nevertheless, he'd been a great dad to me. He'd even adopted me and given me his last name once he and my mom got married. I'd been about five at the time. My parents were pretty laid-back and open minded, but I knew my mom and dad would not be happy to know my first job in L.A. was as an entertainment specialist, whatever that meant.

It was still unclear to me what I would be doing on the island. Gertrude didn't seem to know any more than I did. She was a jolly person, which had surprised me. For some reason, I thought she would be more like the cranky old woman I'd met. The only bad thing about Gertrude was that she was so efficient that just talking to her made me feel inept at life. Within 15 minutes of being on the phone with her, I had my direct deposit set up, room and food preferences noted and all the transportation to and from the island arranged.

Kenny had already left to teach his early morning cycling classes when Richard had called me. I knew Kenny wouldn't have his phone on him, so I'd called Cyril to tell him I was leaving. Cyril had been ecstatic. I hadn't shared with him how much they were going to pay me because I felt he might get suspicious, as I had been. I didn't need him convincing me of someone's nefarious plan to sell me into white slavery or something. To say the least, Cyril could be quite dramatic.

I reached into my purse and pulled out a lip balm. My lips were dry and I knew that was because I was not only parched but nervous. I then reached into my bag for a bottle of water and the other women started moving towards the windows of the exquisite yacht transporting us to the island. I'd never been on a yacht before. My dad loved to go fishing and I'd accompanied him on several fishing trips, but we always rented a small boat. The yacht we were on was easily several million dollars. I figured it belonged to Richard or probably was the property of his company. I wondered if the guests were transported over in a similar fashion. I looked out across the gorgeous blue water as we neared the island. I could see the white sandy beaches from the boat and the lush green landscape went on for miles. A tropical paradise awaited us.

The other girls were giggling and I couldn't help but

share in their excitement. As far as the eye could see, everything was beautiful.

Huge blue umbrellas dotted the coastline and as we approached, I could see the water went from a dark blue to an almost transparent emerald with hints of aquamarine. Even the water looked expensive. Beyond the beaches I could see rows of rich forest, all so green and lush. Within the greenery, barely perceptible, were tree houses the likes of which I'd only ever seen on TV. It was as if someone had built mansions not only among the trees but within the trees themselves.

I started to rethink my "I hate nature" attitude.

We pulled up to the port and made our way down the platform. We were told to leave our luggage on board so that the porter could attend to them. I hadn't felt comfortable with the idea because I hated to be separated from my belongings, but I didn't want to be difficult.

As we all left the ship, someone was approaching us, coming down a path from the forest. The person waved and I realized it was Richard. Happily, I waved back.

"Nina! Of course, you're leading the pack," he said, giving a big grin. He was wearing a loose linen suit and he looked very handsome. I told him so and he gave me a grateful smile. "It's hard to look professional and relaxed at the same time."

The rest of the ladies had caught up with me and so

Richard excused himself and greeted all of them person-
ally as well. I was impressed that he knew us all by
name.

"So, continue up this path to the resort. The on-site
manager will be there to meet you all. Have fun ladies!"
he called, heading towards the yacht.

We did as he said. There was a lot of excited
squeaking and exclamations of "Oh my God, look at
that!" as we made our way to the resort. Various man-
made waterfalls lined the path, making the island seem
like an absolute utopia.

And then we saw the resort. It was a like a giant tree
house, but modern and sleek with walls of windows.

"Wow, just wow," I whispered to myself.

"It's something, isn't it?" said one of the girls, finally
talking to me. "My friend stayed here last week and she
said it's even more impressive inside."

"Your friend works here too?"

"Well, no one really works here. They use different
girls depending on what the client requests."

"Yeah, I knew that," I lied. Now I was even more
curious about what the entertainment specialist position
really entailed.

"No, you didn't," she shot back and I immediately
stiffened up. She noticed my body language and was
immediately apologetic. "Sorry."

"Anyway," I said wishing she would go away, but

figuring she wouldn't now. "Since your friend was here… what do you know about this place? What exactly can we expect? They just keep telling me that we're expected to entertain the guests."

"Yep, that's pretty much it. Except that each entertainment specialist is assigned to one guest."

I glanced at the other girls and said, "Isn't it a bit weird that we're all relatively attractive women?"

"Nope. The clients are mostly rich guys coming here for bachelor parties and stuff."

I groaned. "So I signed up to be a glorified babysitter for a client who will probably think I'm a stripper."

She laughed. "No. These guys are high class. You don't have to worry about that. My friend had the best time. She said all the girls she worked with had the same feedback. The guys go out of their way to please you, so it's almost as if they work for us, not the other way around."

We entered the resort and a short red-head wearing a linen dress and a big sunhat waved at us happily.

"Hi, ladies! I'm Gertrude! Welcome to Solomon's Paradise!" she said, practically bouncing on the balls of her feet. "Come on. Let me show you to your rooms."

We followed behind her. She led us down a hall and then up a staircase made from gorgeous wood. I stroked it lovingly as I walked by.

"Top of the line. We spared no expense," she assured

me with a smile. "Ladies, this wing of the resort is for you only."

She reached into her pocket and pulled out fancy, little envelopes. She started calling our names one at a time and each girl happily grabbed an envelope, found their key and assigned room inside. They were gorgeous rooms. I peeked in every time someone else opened their door.

Finally, I received mine. I was so thrilled, probably even more so than the others. They were probably used to extravagance. I certainly wasn't.

I opened my room and realized that unlike all the others, mine had a view of the forest. It was beautiful. The floor of my room extended into the forest and sat above the trees. If I looked down, it appeared as if my room was part of the nature around me. The architecture was bordering on divine.

I was in awe and apparently so were the rest of the girls who had decided to invite themselves in to stare at my view.

"Oh my gosh! This is sooo nice," one gushed. "You're *so* lucky."

I nodded, speechless. If this was what it felt like to work for the rich, then I should have sought them out a long time ago, I decided.

And then I saw my uniform, which was a long, strapless maxi dress. The bodice featured an intricate white floral detail and the bottom from just above the knee down to the ankles was made from sheer, delicate material. I felt I'd rip it just by touching it.

"Oh my gosh. Your dress is so beautiful. It's like you got the best of everything."

I was confused. "You guys don't have the same dress?"

They all shook their heads. "No, everyone has a different dress. Yours is the only one that is white."

"Maybe you're the virginal sacrifice," one said. A few of the other girls snickered, and Gertrude cleared her throat.

"Leave the cattiness for another day, ladies. It won't be tolerated here. Everyone's here to have a good time. If I even feel that one of you is making life difficult for someone else, I'll have you replaced and you won't be compensated for your time."

I smiled to myself. I liked Gertrude… maybe when I grew up I'd be just like her. I smiled at my thought. I had just turned 22 and Gertrude looked to be around 30. There wasn't a huge gap between us, but I admired how confident and self-assured she was. She was the type of woman who demanded respect and received it. I could learn a lot from her.

"Your assignments are eagerly waiting to meet you all. I would suggest that you get dressed and refreshed quickly." At that moment, the porter came in with my bag and set it on my bed.

I smiled and mumbled thanks, and he gave me a small wave in acknowledgment.

The other girls disappeared and Gertrude along with them.

I freshened up in the bathroom, which was just as fancy as the rest of the room. I applied mascara and eyeliner, hoping to make my already large dark eyes seem even bigger. I was frequently told I had a natural "deer caught in headlights" look. My eyes were my best feature, large and almond shaped like my mother's. I applied a nude lipstick to my full lips and smiled in the mirror. I decided to braid my hair into a goddess braid around my head and took a flower from a vase and stuck it behind my ear.

I inspected myself after I was fully dressed and totally approved. I was a knock out. I was ready to entertain… or be entertained.

I made my way down the hall where an attendant pointed me in the direction of the dining room. When I walked in, I saw the other women from my group already there and there were about five men chatting with them. Waiters bearing food and drinks made their rounds and I nervously reached for a glass of wine, hoping for a little "liquid courage."

I was assigned to G. L. Wallace. That's what the note

had said in my envelope. I nervously approached the group of men who thankfully were wearing name tags. Not one said G. L. Wallace.

Where was my assignment?

And then I noticed a figure standing on the balcony overlooking the jungle. I made my way to the French doors that led to the balcony and stood at the threshold, my heart racing. I didn't know why I was so nervous.

A million thoughts were racing through my mind. What if he didn't like me? What if he thought I was ugly? What if he was ugly? I mean, not unattractive, but an ugly person? Mean and cranky? God, what had I gotten myself into?

As that last thought entered my head, the man turned around and my breath caught.

"G.L. Wallace?" I asked with a shaky voice as I showed him my assignment card.

He gave me a small smile that served to make my pulse quicken, "Griffin. My friends call me Griff. And as luck would have it, you're Parking Lot Girl?"

I laughed nervously. "It's Nina. Nina Charles."

"Nina," he said, putting down the glass of champagne and approaching me. He stopped right in front of me and said, "You're the last person I expected to see here. I thought all the entertainment specialists were going to be sorority sisters. At least that's what the guys told me ad nauseam."

"Definitely not a sorority girl. Disappointed?"

He shook his head slowly, letting his eyes look over me. He took his time, slowly starting at my face and then slowly moving down my body.

I could feel myself blushing as he got an eyeful. My breasts, though on the smaller side, looked huge in the dress I was wearing because of the deep V-neck that left little to the imagination.

While he checked me out, I did the same, I'm not ashamed to admit. It was like heat was filling the space between us as we studied each other. He wasn't dressed as formally as before. This time he wore plain white jeans and a nautical-themed shirt. It was topped with a flawlessly cut white blazer. He looked handsomely untouchable, yet his body language showed he was completely relaxed.

"I hope you approve."

"I do," I said. "You're very attractive when you and your driver aren't trying to run me over."

I expected him to say something equally flirtatious back to me, but he didn't. He was just studying me. I immediately felt a little unsure of myself. Noticing, he quickly reassured me saying, "Don't mind me. I don't know how to flirt. I'm pretty terrible at anything that comes before foreplay."

I opened my mouth and then closed it, not sure what to say. I blurted, "I have no plans to sleep with you."

He arched an eyebrow. "Maybe not now, but eventually."

"Wow, you're arrogant."

"I'm honest."

I tried to be angry, because being angry would allow me to ignore the effect his words had on my body. I could already feel myself growing wet at the thought of being intimate with him. And I knew if I looked down, I would notice that my nipples were now peaked against the fabric of my dress, revealing my desire to let him do exactly what he wanted to every part of my body.

Woah, where had that thought come from? I felt out of my element and nervously fingered my dress.

I vowed to myself that if he noticed my erect nipples, I'd just blame their hardness on the light breeze in the air. He chose to ignore them.

"What do you say we take a walk and get to know each other better? You're supposed to keep me entertained, right?"

"According to the itinerary, we're supposed to have dinner and drinks with the others soon."

He looked towards the room and grimaced. "I don't know about you, but that sounds like torture to me."

I could tell from his face that he meant it. "I don't know," I said with a shrug. "They don't look so bad. They seem friendly enough to me. And aren't they your friends?"

"God, no. They're my brother's friends. His best man backed out or got arrested, or both. I can't remember, so I'm the last-minute fill in to take his place. If I could run away screaming from this place, I would."

It was all starting to make sense. "So, I'm here to replace the girl who should have been here. No wonder the other women were giving me dirty looks. I guessed I replaced their friend. So, let me guess, you like brunettes?" I remembered one of the sorority sisters explaining each girl was matched according to the client's preferences.

"Yep."

"And the others all prefer blondes?"

"I guess. I haven't bothered to ask. I try to talk to them as little as possible."

I laughed again. "It can't be that bad."

"Oh, you're right. It's worse. Their interests include sex, drinking, golf and television."

I giggled again. I loved his frank way of speaking.

"I'll admit I enjoy sex as much as the next person, maybe even more so," he said pointedly giving me a devilish look that made my heart race. "But I hate golf. Beer disgusts me and I rarely have time to watch TV. Clearly, I don't have much in common with my brother and his friends… most of whom are grown men determined to behave like frat boys this weekend. The whole idea of this island is ridiculous and borderline immoral.

I can't believe Richard pulled this off. One woman to meet your every need? I had to double check the legitimacy of the establishment before I agreed to come. I wouldn't put it past my brother to try to arrange an escort for me as a joke."

"Is that how this place is marketed? One woman to meet your every need?" I'd taken a women's studies class during my freshman year of college and I knew my professor wouldn't be pleased if she could see me now.

"Well, those were my brother's words."

"Yikes."

"Tell me about it. I might not be a feminist, but I'm not misogynistic either. The premise behind this place is just creepy."

"Yet, you came…"

"And yet, you work here…"

"Hey, I was hired to be an entertainment specialist."

He laughed then and it caught me off-guard. His laugh was unselfconscious, deep and rich. And I found myself laughing along.

"I'm a glorified Hooters girl, aren't I?"

"Bingo," he said, and I shook my head in disbelief.

"Well, at least the pay is good."

He smiled at me. "That's good to know. I was afraid this whole thing might have been a front for human trafficking."

I giggled. "Are you always this cynical?"

He shrugged. "It's in my nature."

"We'll make quite a pair this week."

"I'm looking forward to it. So how about that walk?"

I looked towards the dining room where everyone was gathering but us, but I didn't feel like they would be even half as much fun as Griffin.

"I'd gladly take you up on that offer."

He took my hand in his and I remembered the other day, how it felt to be comforted by him. Griffin was virtually a stranger to me and I was agreeing to join him on a walk in a strange place. I should have been afraid, or at the very least cautious. But I didn't feel fear… just excitement.

The evening was turning out to be quite an adventure, I thought to myself, as we disappeared through a door and stepped out into paradise.

3

Once we were down the stairs, he let go of my hand. We walked close to each other, not quite touching, but close enough to do so. I felt so unnerved. Reckless abandon wasn't very me, but with Griffin, I was throwing caution to the wind.

"So, you wanted to talk… so let's talk…" I said playfully, even though I was enjoying the silence in his presence.

"Why are you here?"

"It's a job," I said, shrugging. "And I needed a job."

"So, you deliberately signed yourself up for this?"

"That day you saw me, I was actually coming back from my audition as a camp counselor… entertainment specialist… whatever you want to call it."

"They made you audition in your swimsuit? Richard should be ashamed of himself."

I groaned. "I don't have the best of luck in general and the other day was no exception. I was attempting to go to a swimsuit model audition and instead ended up auditioning for this job before almost getting run over by your car."

"You are unlucky."

"Thanks, Griff."

He laughed.

We were suddenly approaching a clearing and I could see the beach beyond the trees.

"Wow, this place is paradise."

"Maybe if I weren't here for a bachelor party I would be inclined to agree with you."

"What's your problem? It's just a group of guys having fun, blowing off some steam before a wedding."

"Sorry, crowds just aren't my idea of a good time."

"There are only about ten people in there."

He grimaced. "That's like a million."

I laughed and he surprised me by sitting down suddenly in the sand and patting the space next to him.

"So, let me guess. You're an introvert?" I said, crouching down next to him.

"I don't like labels."

I rolled my eyes.

"But if I had to be defined, then I guess introvert would be the right word."

"So, what do you do in your free time? Stay inside and read books?"

"Pretty much. And work."

"Fun times."

"I enjoy it," he said dryly.

I decided to change the subject. "Griffin's an unusual name? Is it a family name?"

"It's a nickname."

"So, the G in G.L. Wallace doesn't stand for Griffin?"

"Nope."

"What does it stand for?"

He looked at me with narrowed eyes. "Why do you want to know?"

I shrugged. "Just curious?"

"Are you going to stalk me on social media if I tell you?"

"Do you want me to stalk you on social media?"

He pretended to be pensive, scratching at a non-existent beard. "Maybe, if that's what you're into… don't stop on my account."

He was funny and I couldn't help but laugh even if the joke was at my expense.

"I like your laugh." He smiled down at me and it was then that I realized how close we actually were. I'd given him plenty of room, but unknowingly we'd migrated closer and closer together as we talked.

"Glad it meets your approval."

He reached to touch my face, his hand trailing over into my hair. I rested my face against his palm, feeling close to him and comfortable in his presence. I didn't readily take to most men. In fact, I was normally shy and rebuffed male attention. No matter how arrogant it sounded, being the prettiest girl in school had been more of a headache than anything else, so I tended to downplay my looks.

As a result, I'd had few boyfriends. I had one boyfriend when I was 17 and needed someone to take me to prom and then another boyfriend in my brief time in college, which had been at least three years ago.

"You have such beautiful eyes. They're so unusual," he said.

"Most of the women in my family have eyes like mine."

"Are most of the women in your family as beautiful as you?"

"Yes," I said matter-of-factly. "So don't get any ideas."

"Trust me. I'll try not to hit on your mother."

My laugh was muffled by his lips as he caught me off guard by kissing me softly. He pulled away and said, "I hope this doesn't violate your contract."

"Who cares?" I said bringing his mouth back to mine, kissing him thoroughly.

We broke apart when we heard a strange noise approaching. It was a guy on a golf cart. He waved to us and kept on moving. I assumed he was a security guard of some sort.

"Take off your clothes."

"What?"

"There's a body of water, illuminated by the moonlight. We're two attractive people with no inhibitions."

"No inhibitions? Speak for yourself…" I mumbled.

"Let's go skinny dipping. There's no one here but me and you. Take a chance. Come on."

I shook my head. "I've taken enough chances for one day. After all, I'm here with you, right? A complete stranger. Kissing under the moonlight."

He seemed ready to try to cajole me when we heard voices.

"Looks like someone's coming," I said just before the group rounded the corner.

"There you are! Getting cozy already, I see," said a guy who had clearly already had too much to drink.

Griff ignored him and stood up, offering a hand to help me up.

"Don't leave on our account," said the guy as he slung an arm around the girl next to him who giggled.

"Yeah, come on, Griffin. It's a bachelor party. We're supposed to stay out late, get drunk…"

Griffin didn't even bother to respond. He just coldly regarded the guys until they shut up. Clearly, they were intimidated by Griff.

"Cool it, guys. That's just my big brother for you. He defines his own form of fun." The guy talking now was just as tall as Griff but had sandy blonde hair and a big smile. His eyes were playful as he extended his hand to mine. I shook it as he introduced himself.

"I'm Jackson. Griffin's brother, by the way. We haven't formally met. This is Tim, Gunner, Scott, and Spencer."

I nodded in acknowledgment and smiled a little. The guys were staring at me and Griffin as if trying to figure out what we'd just been up to. The girls looked at me as if they were bored. Apparently, I wasn't too interesting to them.

They were carrying champagne bottles. I guess they intended to continue the party on the beach. I didn't feel like being part of that party…

"I'm going to call it a night. It was a pleasure meeting you all. I'll see you tomorrow."

I glanced at Griffin who looked mildly annoyed. "I'll walk you back to the building."

"No," I said, needing a little distance from him, feeling a little overwhelmed and uncomfortable by the apparent interest in us. "You enjoy the party. I'm going to call it a night."

As I walked through the clearing, I looked over my shoulder and saw Jackson being egged on by his buddies. Griffin stood away from them all.

Everyone was stripping and Griffin looked like he wanted to be anywhere else but there.

I muffled a giggle and happily made my way to my room.

* * *

EVEN THOUGH I'D had an eventful evening, I was up early the next day. Too excited to sleep, I'd had some racy thoughts about Griffin that had made sleeping a little difficult.

I took a shower and found another set of clothes waiting for me in front of my door. It was another dress and it was white…. again. Maybe that sorority girl was right. I was starting to feel like some sort of virginal sacrifice.

This dress was pretty plain, white crochet and sheer, and that's when I realized it was a beach cover-up. Underneath it was a plain white bikini bathing suit. Nothing too racy, so I slid it on.

I found my way to the dining room, which was already set for breakfast. None of the other guests had arrived yet, but that was fine by me. I enjoyed the sound of my own thoughts and I knew I didn't have much in common with the other ladies who I found out were finance majors and seniors in college. I also figured now was as good a time as any to practice my Spanish as I chatted with the hostess.

Griffin took that moment to round the corner. He was wearing shorts and a t-shirt, but still found a way to make it look like the sexiest outfit a man could wear. I was starting to understand, it wasn't the clothes, it was him. He could be wearing a tutu and a fur coat and I would probably still find him the sexiest man in the room. He surprised me by greeting me with a kiss on the forehead. And then he too started chatting with the workers, much more articulate in Spanish than I had been.

Something he said made them laugh and I found myself wishing I'd not dropped my college Spanish class in the middle of the semester.

"Want to join me on the balcony?" I asked him when he was done talking.

"Lead the way," he said, helping himself to more pastries than I thought one person could handle.

When we settled outside I looked pointedly at his plate and said, "Are you seriously going to eat all that?"

"Yes…" he looked up at me and smiled. "Jealous?"

"Very."

He chuckled and said, "I have a sweet tooth… always have."

"Lucky for you, you must also have a high metabolism."

He didn't respond, but instead reached for his phone. "Can you keep a secret?" he asked.

Curious, I nodded. He scrolled through a series of pictures and pulled one up on his phone. It was of a chubby teenager, dressed up in golf clothes, holding a golf club smiling brightly at the camera.

"Who's that?"

"Me."

I stared. And the longer I stared, the more I could see a younger version of Griffin. That teasing smile and the playful eyes confirmed it.

"I hit 13 and the fat just melted away… good for me…."

"I hit 13 and couldn't keep the fat away."

"I can't picture you as a chubby teen."

"Oh, I wasn't, I just grew a butt that stopped fitting into certain pairs of jeans…"

"You have a great butt…. I would know… I checked it out when you walked away last night."

I blushed and shook my head. He was too much.

"How did last night go, by the way?"

He looked pained. "Terrible. Everyone stripped down to their swimsuits and went swimming. Some people weren't even wearing suits. Jackson definitely was. He knows his fiancée would kill him if she found out he was hanging out with some random girl naked. But anyway, then they started singing songs and telling jokes, just having fun." He made a face as if fun was distasteful. "It was terrible. You're lucky you left early."

I couldn't help but laugh. "Sounds like torture."

"You have no idea."

"So, in that picture you were playing golf. Why do you hate it now?"

He grew somber. "I used to play with my father. That was a long time ago. He passed a few months after that picture was taken."

"I'm so sorry."

He shrugged it off. "So am I. He was a great guy. But anyway, tell me about your family. Where are you from, by the way? Your Southern accent is noticeable."

"Georgia… southern Georgia."

"Really? I haven't spent much time down south. I've been to Atlanta, but nowhere else in Georgia. How was it growing up out there?"

"Boring. Hence, why I practically ran to L.A. as soon as I got a chance."

"How are you liking it?"

"It's been a difficult transition. I'd never lived outside of Georgia, but it's been exciting and exhausting. And kind of depressing when I look at prices."

He laughed. "L.A. isn't cheap."

"Says the guy with a driver and a Bentley."

"It comes with the territory," he said.

"Really? And what's the territory?"

Before he could answer, Jackson invited himself to our table. He sat down, tossed his feet in the chair next to me and crossed his arms behind his head.

"Look at you two, all cozy," he said, winking at his brother.

He reached out and tried to take a pastry off Griffin's plate. Griffin knocked his hand away in one smooth motion. Jackson tried again, his eyes twinkling like a bad little brother who found a way to taunt the oldest. This time when he reached out to take a pastry, Griffin kicked the chair out from under him, sending Jackson sprawling to the floor.

I gasped and expected Jackson to be angry, but he was laughing, deep belly chuckling.

"Now, see," he said picking himself up from the ground, "if you hadn't come along, you wouldn't have gotten a chance to do that."

"You're just as annoying now as you were when you were seven."

"Thanks, bro, love you too."

I listened to their banter and found myself wondering what it would have been like to have a sibling. Kenny was the closest thing I had. He was my dad's nephew, but his mom worked a lot so he'd spent most weekends and evenings at our house. And before he had moved out to L.A. to go live with his dad, we had pretty much talked to each other every day. He had been so excited to hear that I was moving to L.A. and had readily extended me an invitation to live in the small apartment complex that he owned. He'd inherited it from his grandmother since he was the only grandchild on his father's side of the family.

Finally, Jackson left, stealing a pastry off his brother's plate and running away laughing.

"It's like you guys are still kids."

"I'm pretty sure we'll be acting the same way well into our 90s."

"I think you're right."

"So, tell me more about yourself, Nina. We were rudely interrupted yesterday. You mentioned that you meant to audition for a swimsuit model position. Is that what you're into? Modeling and acting?"

"I have no interest in being a model and frankly, we both know my butt is too big for that anyway."

"But what a lovely butt it is."

"Thanks, Griffin. You're too kind."

"I know."

I playfully rolled my eyes at him. "So anyway, like I was saying—I'd love to be a professional actress. Drama club was the only thing that held my interest in school. I liked programming too, but I didn't apply myself enough. At least, that's what my teacher said before she sent me to detention for doing absolutely no homework."

"Acting and programming? Those are two very different fields," he commented.

"I know… they're not very similar, but that's what I liked in high school."

"Where'd you go to college?"

That was a sore point for me, but I decided to just be honest. "I went to a state school not far from home. I was two semesters short of graduating but I didn't have the focus for it. I decided to come out here to L.A. and try my hand at acting instead."

"I hope it works out for you. I hope you get to see your name in lights or on Hollywood's Walk of Fame."

"Maybe… maybe one day."

"Have a little faith in yourself, Nina. If you don't have faith in yourself, how are others expected to believe in you?"

I knew he was right. "Self-confidence has never been my strength."

"Just fake it until you make it. Isn't that L.A.'s motto?"

"I can't believe I'm taking advice from a man who eats ten pastries for breakfast."

"Don't judge me," he said jokingly and I laughed. I always found myself laughing in Griffin's presence. I think I was starting to develop a little bit of a crush on him. To be honest, I think it was more than a crush. Not only was I very attracted to him, I liked who he was. I liked his anti-social tendencies. I liked his sense of family responsibility and the way he lived his life by his own set of rules. He had his quirks, but didn't we all?

He was a cool guy and I wondered if maybe he would be interested in getting to know me once we left the island.

As if reading my mind, he said, "I like you, Nina Charles. You're different from most of the women in L.A. that I've known."

"Really, how so?" I tried to act as if his words didn't have an effect on me, but his opinion mattered to me more than I cared to admit.

"You're charming in the most innocent way. You're sweet. You don't laugh at my jokes because you think I want you to. You laugh at them because you genuinely think I'm funny."

"So I'm one of a million girls that actually find you humorous. Go figure."

"These silly L.A. girls just don't get me like you do," he said playfully. He settled back and his expression grew serious. "So, how'd you sleep last night?"

I cleared my throat and said, "Fine. Why?" I could tell from the look in his eyes that the direction of the conversation was changing to a more intimate subject matter.

"I thought about you last night. If Jackson and his crew hadn't come along when they had…"

"Nothing more would have happened," I interrupted, blushing.

"You really believe that?"

I felt a familiar stirring between my legs and crossed one leg tightly over another. "We're in public, let's talk about something else."

He reached under the table and stroked my leg lightly.

"No one's around but us," he said. He continued to stroke my outer thigh. His hand felt warm and I wanted to spread my legs and let his hand explore other areas. I resisted and slapped at his hand.

"Control yourself."

He sighed and pulled his hand back. "I'll do my best, but I'm not going to make any promises." He leaned towards me and whispered softly, "I want you and I know you want me too. It's going to happen between us... it's just a matter of when and where."

He got up then and went to talk to the rest of his brother's crew. I needed a cold shower. I didn't know how I was going to get through the next few hours, let alone the next few days without thinking about his words and how they rocked me to my very core.

I SPENT the next few days avoiding spending any time alone with Griffin. I was afraid that just a few minutes alone with him would end with me in a very compromising position. Thankfully, we didn't have another solo activity until the massage therapists arrived on the island.

Each guest and entertainment specialist was paired up in their own little tent just off the shore. Griffin lay on a table a few feet away from me and after the masseuse left, we continued to lie there looking out at the waves.

I heard Griffin stand up and told myself not to turn around, but I peeked and saw his naked, perfect backside before he slid on his robe. I turned around quickly and pretended to be looking out over the water, but the view of Griffin's backside rivaled the view in front of me.

"We should get going," I said at last, not really meaning it. "I'm sure they're waiting for us." I sat up on the table and absent-mindedly made sure my robe was still tied.

Griffin stopped in front of me. I sat there facing him, knowing that my resolve was slowly fading away. I could see the evidence of his desire clearly pressing against his robe, and I could feel the evidence of my desire starting off as a dull ache between my legs.

"They can wait," he said reaching towards me and

unknotting the robe I had surreptitiously slipped into once the masseuse exited the tent.

He pushed it down my shoulders and I shrugged it off, not bothering to pretend anymore. He was right. It was going to happen between us eventually, no matter what. And it was happening now.

I hadn't bothered to put my bra back on after the masseuse left. My breasts were exposed and Griffin slowly brought them into his hands, cupping them. He brushed my nipples with his thumbs and I sighed in pleasure, enjoying the feel of his warm hands against my breasts, touching my nipples, making me moan.

"Shhh..." he said, kissing me hard to silence me. "We don't want to get caught."

He grabbed my hand and we sneaked around the other tents. My heart was racing in anticipation. We made our way up a staircase that I didn't even know existed. It led to what I guessed was the other wing of the resort.

"Just up these stairs," he said.

As I went up, I could feel his hand sliding up my leg. I immediately paused and turned around.

"I don't think we're going to make it to the room... I want you now, Griffin," I said, not caring if we got caught screwing like a pair of horny teenagers on the stairs.

"There's a supply closet off the kitchen," he said as he

turned me back around and pressed against me. I could feel his erection against my butt and I shifted against it, teasing him.

"Stop teasing me or I'll take you right here, right now on these stairs."

I pressed my butt up against his penis again and he promptly slid a hand between my legs when we heard voices echoing in the staircase.

"Supply closet it is," he said simply, moving his hand away from my warmth. My heart was beating and I felt an overwhelming sense of urgency as if I had to have him inside me, right there and then. I felt like waiting would make me explode.

"Right here," he said, as I accidentally passed the closet by. I backtracked quickly and went in. He followed me inside and closed the door securely behind us. I dropped the robe and he dropped his. He backed me up against a wall and then easily picked me up and wrapped my legs around his hips. My legs were open just enough for him to enter me and he did so without hesitating. He slid into my wetness easily, filling me with one single smooth motion.

I groaned as he began to pound into me and I wrapped my arms around his neck. Each of his thrusts into my wetness made me gasp and my back hit against the wall as he pushed in and out of me.

I wanted him deeper though, and I pushed against

him in frustration, not yet feeling bold enough to tell him what I wanted.

"You want me to stop?" he asked confused, panting, searching my face with his eyes.

"No… don't stop." And so he didn't as he pushed in and out of me.

I came hard, quick, gasping for breath. My legs quivered around his hips, but as he was close to coming he abruptly pulled out.

"Why'd you stop?" I demanded.

"Condom… I forgot about a condom…"

In the sexual haze, I'd forgotten all about protection.

"In your room?"

He shook his head. "I didn't plan to get laid on this trip."

I groaned and he helped me put my robe back on. He pressed his room key into my hand. "I have a private suite off the resort. Stop by tonight, I'm sure I can raid one of the guys' rooms for a condom."

"Ok. What time?"

"Midnight. How does that sound?"

"Too long to wait."

He laughed. "Get out of here before I ruin your reputation."

He swatted me on the butt and I made my way out of the supply closet looking left then right, hoping that no one spotted me.

4

———

That evening was so hard to get through. I dressed carefully in another white dress they'd given me, but I decided to forego a bra. I let my hair down so it spilled across my shoulders and I applied a light shade of lipstick.

I wanted him so bad, I couldn't concentrate on anything else.

I didn't know how the food tasted. I barely gave any answers to any questions. I was so aware of him. I remembered the feel of him inside me. God, how I wanted him.

Finally, when midnight came around, I entered his suite and saw him sitting on the bed waiting for me. He was wearing nothing but his boxer briefs. His perfect abs seemed to tempt my eyes lower and lower. As he came closer to me, I noticed how beautiful his legs were.

He had strong muscular legs, perfectly proportional to the rest of his muscular, hard body.

He slid his hands up my arms. Just the feeling of his hands made me shake even though his touch wasn't provocative at all.

I couldn't say the same for his look, as he slid his hands under the spaghetti straps of my dress and watched the dress pool around my ankles.

He took a step back, allowing me room to step out of it.

He stared at me, not touching me at first, and then slowly he took my hand to lead me to his bed and lie me down. He took that moment to step out of his briefs. He was hard, ready for me.

He parted my thighs with a hand and trailed a finger across my sex. My hips rocked upwards to meet his fingers. He put his head between my legs and began to lick me through the fabric of my panties that were already starting to grow wet at his attention.

He pushed my panties to the side and began to slide one finger at a time in and out of me. I spread my legs wider and began to pant, unable to catch my breath.

"Griffin…" I moaned.

He stopped abruptly to slowly pull my panties down my legs before tossing them to the floor.

He finally reached for a condom and I parted my legs

wide, looking up at him in anticipation as I watched him sheath himself.

To my surprise, he didn't push into me. Instead he buried his head between my legs again and lazily traced circles around my clit. I screamed this time. I couldn't control it. The pleasure was too great.

He attempted to shush me again, but I was beyond reason. I didn't care who heard me as I moaned over and over again.

He stopped and picked me up around my waist, and we swapped places. I found myself on top of him while he lay underneath me. I thought he wanted me to ride him, so I moved to mount him when he pulled me further up, past his pelvic bone, across his chest, until my legs were on either side of his face.

I didn't understand what he wanted until he lowered my hips so they were just above his face and started to lick me.

I planted my hands against the headboard. My thighs quivered as he ate me out. He was relentless, taking what he wanted, using his hand to penetrate me while allowing his mouth and tongue to lick and suck.

I rode his face, gasping. Finally, I let go of the headboard as he anchored my hips and I began to play with my nipples. I pretended my hands were his hands. And shortly after, I came hard, covering Griffin's lips with my wetness.

As I anchored my hands against the headboard, coming down from my orgasm, I realized that Griffin was watching my face while touching himself. He was stroking his manhood up and down and I wanted him inside me so bad.

I climbed off him and he looked puzzled. "Don't want to be on top?"

I shook my head and got on all fours in front of him.

"What a beautiful ass," he said, before I felt him getting up behind me.

I stretched my hands out in front of my body and placed my breasts against the mattress. My hips were up in the sky and I could feel his dick pressing against my behind. He teased me again, tracing my outer lips with his dick while rubbing my clit.

"Put it in…" I moaned.

"Shhh…"

"Put it in, please, Griffin…"

"As you wish," he said softly, as his hands came up to either side of my behind and I could feel him opening me a little more as he slid slowly, inch by inch, into me.

I felt my insides stretching, adjusting to his welcomed invasion. I was gasping, breathing heavily, ready to come again when he stopped taking his time and pushed into me.

"Griffin!" I screamed over and over. I wasn't thinking and I didn't care who heard us.

"Deeper?"

"Yes," God, yes.

"Faster?"

"Please."

I gasped as he began to pound into me again. His thrusts were pushing me forward and I grabbed the foot of the bed, trying to steady myself.

As I did, he pulled out slowly, leaving only the tip of his dick as he pushed back into me.

"How's that feel?" he asked between breaths.

Amazing, I wanted to say, but I was too gripped by pleasure to talk. He stretched me, filled me, and my sex embraced him like he was the answer to all my problems.

I grew wetter and wetter as he thrust into me, changing the depth and rhythm of his thrusts periodically. I had thought the experience in the closet had been mind-blowing, but what he was doing to me at that moment rendered me unable to think. I could only feel and what I felt was his warm thickness moving in and out of me. The pace was almost hypnotic. I wanted even more of him even though he was already inside of me.

I pushed my hips back against him and I heard him moan. I did it again and was rewarded by another moan.

"You're going to make me come," he gasped.

"Good," I managed to breathe.

He grabbed my hips then and quickened his pace. He

was so deep inside of me that just another fraction of an inch would have hurt.

I knew I was about to come again as he pulled out and my walls tightened around him, making his entry and exit difficult. I was massaging his dick with my pussy and apparently he liked it.

"Fuck me harder," I said to him, surprising myself.

But he didn't question me. He did what I asked, riding me hard, pushing in deep. When I came, he came too, with a hoarse shout that was my name.

I slumped forward in the afterglow of orgasm, moaning a little as my sex clenched and unclenched around Griffin's length.

Instead of collapsing next to me, he picked me up and placed my head on a pillow and lay next to me. He gave me a kiss on my cheek and I settled into a deep sleep. The only thing on my mind was the perfect man lying next to me.

I don't know how long I slept but when I woke up I realized the sun was up. I was a little embarrassed for sleeping too long.

"You should have woken me up," I said to Griffin as I turned over, except Griffin wasn't there.

I sat up and looked around. His bedroom looked

very different in the light. In the dark, I didn't know how beautiful it was. In the light, the opulence was painfully noticeable. I'd thought my room had been impressive, but it might as well have been a cheap room in a motel in comparison to Griffin's.

I wondered not for the first time how much this island cost for the week.

But I pushed those thoughts aside as I put my clothes back on and looked for Griffin. I expected to see him in the opulent bathroom, but he was nowhere to be found.

I didn't know what time it was, but I knew it had to be around seven given where the sun was.

I slowly opened the door and let myself out of his room, only to run right smack into someone's chest.

That someone was Jackson.

"Hey, Nina…" He looked a little nervous.

"Hi, Jack, have you seen your brother?" I didn't see the point in pretending that I hadn't spent the night with him.

Jack looked ready to bolt and my stomach dropped. Why would Jack be afraid to talk to me?

I gulped. "Let me guess, he's no longer on the island and he sent you here to do his dirty work."

Jackson ran his hand through his hair. "I'm sorry, Nina. I know this looks bad, but—"

I was tearing up and I struggled to maintain control

of my voice. "It's ok. It's not your fault. I think I'll be leaving too. Do you know who I can talk to?"

Jack looked ashamed. "It's all been arranged. Gertrude already knows and made arrangements for you. But it's not what you think—"

"Don't cover for him, Jackson. It's exactly how it looks." I wanted to get as far away from Jackson as I could. I needed to remove myself from the situation. I was hurting. How could Griffin do this to me?

"He had an emergency come up…"

"It's ok, you don't have to lie for him, Jackson."

"It's not a lie, my brother's not a liar," Jackson said, more to himself than to me.

I was done listening and walked off. Jackson followed behind me.

"Nina, I know this looks bad, but my brother genuinely likes you. I'm sure he'll make this up to you."

"Yeah, sure," I said pitifully, wiping at my eyes. To my chagrin, the staff seemed to be interested in the public scene unfolding in front of them.

"Look, he told me to give you his card," he said with a hint of desperation. I guess Jackson was a genuine guy… unlike his brother. I took the card out of his hand and ripped it up. I was enraged.

He watched, open-mouthed, and then tried to stop me. He froze when I glared at him and took a step back.

"I'm leaving. Now. Give your brother my regards, wherever he may be."

And with that I stomped off. I kept my bravado up to the point when I reached my room. It was then that I allowed myself to breakdown. I was just happy I'd kept it together that long.

I hadn't been with many men and I certainly didn't jump into bed with just anyone. I'd thought Griffin was special, but apparently he was a piece of crap. I'd let the romance of the island and the circumstances of how we met cloud my judgment.

I wanted to go home. And I didn't just mean Kenny's apartment. I meant Georgia. I wanted to get as far as possible from Griffin and the reminder of how Griffin had walked away and left me like I was some sort of cheap whore.

At that moment, I looked in the mirror and saw the dress that before looked alluring, now suddenly looked slutty. I flung it off and put on my own clothes.

I grabbed my bag with my meager belongings and walked out the door. I didn't have a plan other than to wait at the pier until the yacht came for me. Someone would come for me eventually. The girls and the other guys were gathered around having a laugh about some-thing and they were caught off guard as I went stomping through their group not bothering to say a word.

"What's up with her?" I heard one of them say. I was

sure my exit would give them tons of juicy gossip while they remained on the island. And I didn't really care. I had to get out of there.

I then heard footsteps behind me. It was Jackson. Again.

"I'm fine. Go away."

"It's my brother. I have him on the phone, he wants to speak to you."

"Tell him to go screw himself."

He handed me his phone and I don't know what got into me, but I threw it. Straight into the bushes.

"Hey! I just bought that."

"Well, now you can buy another. Have a great wedding, Jackson."

I left him walking through the bushes trying to retrieve his phone. I didn't feel sorry in the least. He might have lost a phone that day, but I had lost my heart.

A month and a half later, I sat on my mom's front porch. She and my stepdad lived in a lovely neighborhood. I never really appreciated it until that moment.

"This was a great place to be a kid," I said to her, avoiding the conversation I knew she wanted to have.

She had been the first one to notice the slight changes. After things went sour with Griffin I'd gone home to lick my wounds. I felt silly that a man could make me feel so bad. But he had.

I told Kenny I'd be back shortly. But what was

supposed to have been only a few weeks turned into over a month. I was depressed and feeling listless. I knew I needed to try harder to be more resilient, but I tended to give up on things easily.

But I wouldn't be allowed the luxury of that flaw anymore, I thought to myself, as I swung on the porch swing with Mom. In between us sat a little white plastic stick that told me I was pregnant.

"You know you can stay here as long as you want."

I turned to look at her, full of love and gratitude. She was just an older version of me. We had the same color hair, the same color eyes… I briefly wondered if the child I was carrying would look like us too. But I couldn't focus on such inconsequential things. I had to focus on what my mother was saying. I needed her now.

Her words meant a lot to me. She didn't care that I was having a kid out of wedlock, no matter how conservative a town we lived in. My mother was a special woman who made her own rules and one day I hoped to make her proud.

"Thanks for that, Mom. I think I'll need to take you up on that offer, at least until I get back on my feet." I laughed bitterly. "Pregnant and unemployed at the ripe old age of 22. I sure know how to be successful, don't I?"

"Don't beat yourself up. Life's a whirlwind, Nina. You never know what it has in store for you. You just have to roll with the punches or at least fight back."

I needed to start learning how to fight. I had a lot to learn about life, about motherhood, and she was the best person I knew to teach me. I knew she'd be supportive of me, she always was. But part of me didn't want her understanding. I wanted her to sound disappointed in me because I was disappointed in myself.

A long moment passed and then she said, "Are you going to contact the father?"

I nodded. "After the baby's born. I don't have the strength to really deal with it before then."

I didn't know if I could handle Griffin's rejection again. I wanted to focus on the child growing inside of me and I didn't want to deal with the stress of Griffin's reaction. Not that I could guess how he would react. I hadn't guessed he'd leave me after making love to me.

Truth be told, I didn't even know how to contact him if I tried. My only contact with him had been on the island and we'd been too busy doing other things to ever exchange phone numbers. I didn't even know his real name. I felt like such a cheap floozy. How could I not even know the name of the father of my child?

"Don't be too hard on yourself," my mom said yet again. "You'll do fine."

"I hope so. I have a great example."

She squeezed my hand and went back inside. I folded my arms around my waist, giving myself a hug. I heard footsteps behind me expecting mom again, but it was my stepdad.

"How ya doing, angel?"

I attempted to smile, but failed. I shrugged. "Not too great, Dad."

He nodded. "Well, you're not going to feel any better moping around here. Let's go build something."

"Let's go build something" was his motto every time I felt like crap. I wanted to tell him no. I wanted to tell him that he couldn't comfort me through this as he had comforted me through childhood troubles, but the words froze in my throat. Maybe I did need to distract myself.

"Lead the way, Dad," I said.

He smiled up at me proudly and I followed him towards his work shed. As we went, I looked at my old swing that still sat in the backyard. I looked out over the hillside where I used to run after butterflies and suddenly the butterflies in my stomach stopped fluttering. I no longer felt sick to my stomach. Maybe it would all be ok. Maybe, just maybe, being a mom would be something I'm good at. I touched my stomach, this time seeing promise instead of failure.

"Don't worry little one, I won't fail you."

I shrugged off my fear and made a commitment to myself and to my baby to succeed. I didn't know how to define success, but for my baby I was going to make it.

"I hope you're ready for an adventure, little one."

I shoved my bitterness and resentment towards Griffin out of my head. I wasn't going to dwell on the pain. After all, it was a one night stand. It wasn't love. At least that's what I was going to keep telling myself until the pain either subsided or life became too busy that I would just simply have to ignore it.

# PART 2

Obstacles

5

I looked at my belly in the mirror. I turned to the side and sighed and then turned back to the front. At three months along, I was barely showing, but my pants were uncomfortable around the waistband. I felt bloated all the time and had terrible heartburn. I ignored all that and made myself stop staring at my body in my bedroom mirror.

I was still at my parents' house. I'd been hiding with my tail between my legs for much too long and today was the day. I'd changed my mind about contacting Griffin. I'd done some legwork and found the contact information of Richard, the guy who'd hired me. I planned to call him today and inquire about Griffin. I wasn't sure if legally he would be able to connect me with him, but I didn't think it would hurt to try.

I sat down on the edge of my bed, pushed the hair out of my face and made the call.

"Hello, Island Associates, this is Lorelei. How can I help you?"

"Hi, Lorelei. I'm actually trying to contact the guy who hired me. I was one of the entertainment specialists and just have a quick question for him." That question being, can you tell me where my baby's daddy is, I thought to myself.

"That would be Mr. Hayes," she replied happily.

"Yes," I said totally not knowing what I was talking about. I realized that up to that moment I hadn't ever bothered to ask his full name. I guessed it was Richard Hayes.

"I can see if he's in. Can I ask who's calling?"

"Nina Charles."

"Nina Charles. Let me see if he's in."

She put me on hold and for some reason, I was nervous. I didn't even have time to analyze why when suddenly Lorelei was back.

"Give me one second and I'll transfer you."

"Oh! Thank you!"

A second later, Richard greeted me warmly. "Nina! How are you? I wanted to reach out to you after your abrupt departure from the island, but I didn't think a call from me would be appreciated." He sounded nervous and I was confused as to why and then it hit me.

"I'm not going to sue you or anything like that. Nothing happened out there that was lawsuit or criminal charges worthy, trust me."

He sighed. "I know, but I still feel guilty. I mean, I don't know what exactly happened between you and Mr. Wallace, but I did feel partially responsible for your abrupt departure."

"You're a nice guy, Mr. Hayes. I was actually calling to see if you could put me in touch with Mr. Wallace."

He coughed, startled. "I'm afraid not. We're not allowed to give out any information about our guests."

"I figured as much."

"Yes, I'm sorry about that. I can't give out his phone number or any contact information at all. I can't even tell you that you can find him at the corporate headquarters in the Westmore building most weekends."

I smiled to myself and quickly reached for a pen.

"I can't tell you that if you go this weekend, you won't have to worry about five different security guards finding you. In fact, the only guard you'll have to worry about is Cliff. Tell him that you're there to see Griff and that Richard sent you."

"How do you know all this?"

"Don't worry about it. Go get him. Good luck, Nina."

We said our goodbyes and hung up. I stared at the

information in my hand and then decisively reached for my computer. Less than ten minutes later, I was scheduled for a flight back to L.A.

I stood up and planted my hands on my waist, feeling in control of my life for the first time since I found out I was pregnant. And then I promptly dropped my hands as a bout of nausea hit me that could only mean one thing: it was time to hug the toilet bowl again. So maybe I wasn't in complete control of my life yet.

* * *

A FEW DAYS LATER, I caught a ride straight from the airport to the Westmore Building. It was an impressive skyscraper that was ultra-modern and ultra-chic.

I nervously walked in and was surprised to see so many people working. I scanned the lobby for the security guard, Cliff, expecting a 60-year-old man with a potbelly and a sour demeanor.

I was so wrong.

Cliff was tall and willowy and looked to be maybe 20 at most. He saw me and gave me a wave.

"Are you Nina?"

"Mr. Hayes, err Richard, told you I was coming, I see."

"Yep. Are you a gamer too?"

I hadn't figured Richard for a gamer, but what did I know?

"Not quite. Cliff, I'm here to see Mr. Wallace."

He nodded. "I'll call his office now."

A minute later I was heading up the elevator on my way to see Griffin. I was proud of myself for having gotten this far. This had been a piece of cake. But as the elevator reached its destination, my confidence dropped with every passing floor. I was nervous. Scared. What if he kicked me out? What if he didn't want anything to do with me or the baby? What if he didn't want the baby? I felt as if my heart was in my throat as I thought about all those scenarios.

The elevator reached my floor and I walked out feeling emotional, and ready to run away. I took a deep breath, squared my shoulders and walked straight into the office.

"I'm here to see, Griff—Mr. Wallace, please."

The assistant, another young guy, reached for the phone and said, "There's a young lady by the name of—" He paused, covered the phone and said, "What's your name again"

"Nina."

"There's a Nina here wanting to speak with Mr. Wallace."

"Ok...ok..." He frowned and listened some more. He looked up at me then with sad eyes. "I'll tell her."

"Mr. Griffin is currently taking a very important call."

"Oh," I said, no longer nervous, just disappointed and irritated. I didn't come all this way for this. "But I was told to come up here by Cliff. He told me Mr. Wallace was available."

"Yeah, that was me who Cliff spoke to. There was nothing on Mr. Wallace's calendar, so I thought he would be able to see you." He gave me an apologetic look. "I'm so sorry, miss. Maybe you can come back later?"

"Come back later? You think it's that easy?" I found myself feeling so annoyed that I wanted to scream. "This… this… this is unacceptable!" I knew I sounded like an old, cranky school teacher, but I was mad. I was beyond mad, I was furious.

"What is unacceptable is you coming in here and making a scene. Now I suggest you leave, or I'll have security escort you out."

I turned around slowly, immediately recognizing that condescending tone, her grating voice. Her presence irritated me even more. It was the grouchy woman from my interview. What was she doing here?

"You!" we both said at the same time, clearly not happy to see each other. Apparently, she disliked me as much as I disliked her.

"What are you doing here? You're that sequins bikini girl!" she scoffed.

"She's here to see Griff—"

"That's Mr. Wallace to you," she growled at the receptionist who looked ready to hide under his desk.

"I need to talk to Griffin. It's a personal matter," I said shortly. I felt intimidated by her but I was determined not to show it. Too much was at stake and she fancied herself some sort of gate keeper to Griffin.

"Whatever you need to speak to Griffin about, you can tell me."

Before pregnancy, I would have just walked away like a coward, but not today. I had too much to lose. I shook my head. "I would prefer to speak to Griffin only, please."

She stared at me and looked me over with disapproval and hostility practically radiating from her pores. I felt that my very presence offended her deeply. She clearly hated me, but she had no reason to. She didn't even know me. I don't know why, but I felt like crying. She was looking at me as if I were some sort of stray dog dragged in from the outside. I felt my resolve disappearing and I struggled to keep my emotions from spiraling out of control.

With a shaky voice, I said again, "I would like to speak to Griffin, please."

"Again, young lady, I told you that won't be possible. Griffin's away on business."

"The receptionist just told me that he's taking a call," I said, trying but failing to stop my voice from betraying my topsy-turvy emotions. I was feeling angry and upset, and barely able to speak.

"The receptionist lied," she stated flatly.

The receptionist opened his mouth to protest and she shot him a steely look that made him openly flinch. It was clear to me the receptionist wasn't the one who was lying.

I decided then to take a stand.

I looked around and sat on the couch nearest. It was one of those stupid, uncomfortable modern couches that were more pieces of abstract art than furniture. I was probably sitting on a sculpture that wasn't furniture, but I wasn't going to move now. It was too late. I was taking a stand, albeit by sitting down. I folded my arms across my chest and stared at the odd piece of art in front of me. Oh jeez, I thought to myself, maybe that was actually the sofa.

"What are you doing?" she asked.

"I'm going to sit here until one of you gets Griffin," I said, trying to sound like I actually meant it. "And I'm not leaving until I see him."

"Very well," the woman said. And without missing a beat, she followed with, "Zach, call security."

"Mrs. Wallace…" Zach said giving me a mournful look. "She's harmless. I mean just look at her. She's sitting on the sculpture for God's sake. Maybe she just needs *help*." The way he said the word "help" made me realize that he thought I had some sort of mental illness. Great. Just great. But whatever. If that worked in my favor, Zach the receptionist could believe anything he wanted.

"Useless," she growled at him. She shoved him away from the desk and proceeded to call security.

Sweat began to pool down my back and my underarms. My heart was racing. What the hell do I do now? I can't get arrested, I thought in panic. I'm pregnant!

Desperate, I tried one more time to talk reason to her. I tried to keep my voice calm even though I felt like crying and shouting in anger at the same time. "Listen, I just need to talk to Griffin. Just five minutes, please. Like Zach said, I'm harmless."

"Security is on its way," she said dismissively.

And she was right. Seconds later two guards showed up at the door.

"Miss, come with us."

I stood up slowly and extended my wrists. I closed my eyes, waiting for them to put the cuffs on me. When nothing happened, I slowly opened my eyes and saw that the security guards were looking at me with a bemused expression.

One shook his head in confusion, hit my hand out the way, and grabbed my arm. "Let's go…"

"Am I being arrested?" I asked, frightened as they escorted me out of the office. I glanced back at Zach and the old woman right as the door closed. The old woman had a small smile on her face and Zach looked like he was ready to cry.

Oh, God. I hope I didn't get him fired, I thought mournfully.

The security guards didn't say a word to me during the elevator ride down. I stood between them awkwardly wondering if a patrol car would be waiting for me downstairs. If I went to jail, I hoped they would allow me to have frequent bathroom breaks because I could barely hold it nowadays.

I started crying at the thought of being pregnant and alone and in jail. Pretty soon, I was sobbing in the elevator and the security guards avoided making eye contact with me.

"Come on," the other one said as they pulled me out of the elevator. My legs were wobbly and I felt like I was going to faint. "No one's going to arrest you. Just calm down."

"Are you—are—are you sure?" I managed to squeak out between deep breaths and sobs.

"Jesus, lady. Get it together," said the other guard. "You can't stalk people without consequences, you know."

"I'm not a stalker!" I said more loudly than I intended.

And then I felt a hand at my elbow. I looked behind me and it was Cliff.

"I'll take it from here, fellas."

One of the security guards patted me awkwardly on the shoulder as if to reassure me. "Listen, you seem like a nice girl. Find a nice boyfriend or girlfriend and get some help."

He walked away with the other security guard and I watched them in silence as they disappeared.

"That was a disaster," I said, tearing up again as Cliff guided me by my elbow out of the building.

"Listen, I'm sorry for what happened back there. I didn't know the old witch was upstairs. She must have used the private executive entrance and didn't notify anyone," Cliff said.

"Who is she?" I asked, still shaken up.

"Mr. Wallace's mother."

"Ohhh…"

"Look, if you give me your phone number and contact information, I'll get it to Mr. Wallace."

I hugged him abruptly, driven to uncustomary displays of affection because I was so grateful for his help. I began to cry again as I hugged him. "Thank you so much. Thank you. Thank you. You're a really great person."

He pried himself out of my arms and said with a soft chuckle. "Hey, not a problem. So, stop all the crying, ok?"

I nodded and wiped at my tears. He pulled a couple of questionable looking napkins out of his pocket. "Here, wipe your face. You have some…" He gestured to my nose.

He didn't have to finish his sentence as I wiped at my nose and thanked him again. I realized that I probably looked a mess. No wonder the security guards thought I was a crazed stalker.

"Anyway, I need to get back in before the old witch notices I'm gone."

He programmed my number into his phone and wished me good luck.

As I sat on the corner, waiting for a bus to take me to my cousin's home, I didn't feel lucky at all.

I LOOKED around the small ice cream shop that sat across from the beach. There were several families milling around and little kids darted in and out. Some collided with each other and moms spent most of their time apologizing to other moms for the actions of their rambunctious children. I hoped that I didn't look like a weirdo staring at them, but they all seemed so happy whilst I was sitting there miserable.

I nervously tapped my finger against the table and with my other hand I played with the straw in my milkshake. I guess my fidgeting bothered the guy across from me as he looked up from the book he was reading, looked at my finger pointedly and then glared at me before burying his nose back into his book.

I gave him an apologetic smile and placed my hands in my lap. I leaned forward and took a big sip of my milkshake, and tried to focus on anything but how nervous I felt.

The day after being escorted from the office, I'd received a phone call from Zach telling me that Mr. Wallace would meet me at 1:00 pm at this location. I'd been so torn. Part of me had been ecstatic that Cliff had come through for me, but the other part of me was terrified about seeing Griffin alone again.

I watched the door as I sat drinking my milkshake. I'd arrived half an hour before the agreed time and had seen a lot of customers come and go.

I watched as a family came in with a little girl, around three years old. She was adorable. She wore a summer hat and a cute sundress. She waved to me as she walked by and I waved back wondering what it would be like to have a little girl of my own. I'd find out soon enough, I thought, feeling a little overwhelmed. The idea of being a mom filled me with panic, but also joy. I looked down at my stomach, which barely showed even a slight bump, and rubbed it without thinking.

It was then that I heard someone in front of me clear their throat. I snatched my hand away from my stomach and looked up. And then I promptly began to choke on the remaining milkshake in my mouth as I saw who had joined me. Mrs. Wallace, my unexpected guest, responded by thumping me hard on the back. I wasn't sure if she had been trying to help me or kill me.

I tried to stop coughing and reached blindly for a glass of water while Mrs. Wallace seated herself across from me. She stared at me as I tried to control my coughing, but offered no further assistance. In fact, she looked bored. She wore a pants suit that looked like it cost several thousand dollars. Her makeup was perfect, and her hair was down for the first time since I'd met her. It was long and a deep chestnut brown without a hint of gray. Either she had no worries or an excellent stylist. I figured it was the latter.

Even after I stopped coughing, I didn't say anything. I was in shock. What was she of all people doing here? Obviously, she'd found out about my conversation with Cliff or maybe my conversation with Zach? Or had she been responsible for the phone call I received from Zach? And then something dreadful occurred to me.

What if Griffin had sent her? No… I didn't think that was what happened. Granted, I didn't really know him all that well, but he didn't come across as the type of guy who would do that. It was too cowardly. No, if Griffin wanted to blow me off, he would have done it himself.

"What are you doing here?" I managed to squeak out finally.

She reached into her purse, pulled out a piece of paper and slid it across the table towards me.

I barely glanced at the paper. "I'm not sure who you think you are, but you have no right to interfere."

"I have every right to protect myself and my family from predators like you."

"Predator?" I said in disbelief. It hurt that she thought so poorly of me. "I'm not a predator. Everything that happened between me and Griffin was—"

She held up a hand. "Please spare me your sordid lies."

"Sordid! Listen, I've had enough of you. I'm not sitting around listening to this."

I stood up and she did too, grabbing the piece of paper on the table and thrusting it into my hand.

"That's 250,000 dollars. I don't care what you do with it, just stay away from my son."

I looked down at the check in my hand and couldn't believe all the zeros. My heart skipped a beat as I thought of a million and one ways I could use the money. Apparently, I had stared a bit too long because Mrs. Wallace had a small smile on her face once I finally looked up. Actually, it was more of a smirk. As if she knew all along that she could easily buy me. I tried to give it back to her but she stepped away from me.

"Take your money. I don't want it."

"Of course you do. You're an out of work actress. You're unemployed and living with your parents and sometimes your cousin."

She'd had me investigated. I felt anger towards her for violating my privacy. No one had a right to do that. She'd gone too far.

"I don't want or need your money," I said coldly, my voice shaking. I felt nauseous, but I wasn't going to show weakness around this woman. I said with conviction that I didn't actually feel, "I'm going to reach Griffin. And you can't stop me. It's not illegal to speak with him."

I could feel the tension between us as she carefully considered her next words. Her eyes flashed with anger, but she managed to control herself. She took a deep breath and gave me a tight smile. "Then go speak to him. He's right across the street."

I stared at her, not believing that she was telling the truth, and she smiled tightly again. "Trust me. He's right outside. If you want to go talk to him… go do it."

"I will," I said decisively.

I turned away and marched out the door. I heard her coming behind me and I ignored her as I scanned the beach in front of me.

I saw him then. He had his hands on his hips, wearing swim trunks and a plain white t-shirt. I couldn't help myself, I smiled upon seeing him again... completely forgetting my reason for needing to speak with him. He looked so attractive and happy.

I moved toward him and noticed that something to his left had caught his attention. And then I saw them. A tall, attractive, young lady and a little girl. They were waving to him and he smiled and moved in their direction. He picked up the little girl and spun her around. She seemed to be about four. He placed her down and bent to tickle her while smiling up at the woman who beamed down at him. They walked away together, Griffin holding one of the little girl's hands and the woman holding the other. They continued to walk down the beach, the little girl happily skipping along between them.

"Is that his family?" I asked softly, ignoring the pain in my gut that made me feel as if I had just been kicked in the stomach.

She nodded and said, "That's my granddaughter, clearly."

"So, he's married, with a family?" I forced myself to ask.

"I'm sorry," she said in response, but she didn't sound sorry. She sounded satisfied. And why shouldn't she be? She'd gotten exactly what she wanted.

I didn't want to believe what I was seeing. And I forced myself to think of any explanation. Something else, anything else. But I watched him playfully toss the kid onto his shoulders and then toss an arm around the shoulders of the woman. They were clearly a family and I felt like a voyeur, an intruder.

I turned away, not saying another word to Mrs. Wallace. I hurt so much, I could barely breathe and I didn't want her to see me like that. I didn't realize until I almost ran into someone that I was crying. I made it about a block before I couldn't see any longer because that's how fast my tears were flowing. I found a bus stop and sat there and sobbed. I must have been loud as even the nearby homeless people moved away from me.

I didn't care that I was making a scene as I buried my hands in my face and let it all out. I was disappointed in myself. I felt dirty. I was an adulterer. I was a terrible person. And now I was pregnant by a man who already had a family. I'd just been his entertainment. I laughed bitterly to myself. After all, wasn't I supposed to be an entertainment specialist?

I felt someone tug at my sleeve and it was the little girl I'd seen previously at the ice cream shop.

"Here," she said handing me a tissue. "My momma said you could probably use this right now."

I realized her mom was standing next to me. "Whatever it is, it'll get better," she said simply before giving me a kind smile and taking her daughter by the hand and walking away.

Her daughter looked back and gave me a small wave, I waved back to her. She turned away and her mom smiled down at her. I stared at them until they were out of my view and suddenly I didn't feel as scared anymore. I had to move on from the pain and move forward. Life was moving forward and, whether I liked it or not, I had to make a choice. I could wallow in self-pity and uncertainty, or I could grow up and be the person I needed to be for my daughter. The type of person who didn't sit crying at a bus stop.

I wiped my nose and buried the pain, at least for now. It was time to stop with the self-pity. Hadn't it been Griffin himself who'd told me to be more confident? And if I didn't feel confidence, that I should fake it? That's what I decided to do. I ignored the self-pity that clawed at me like a bad stomach bug and made a promise to myself that I would do what I needed to do to provide for myself and my daughter. I was like a single tree being blown around by a tornado, but I had to stand strong for my daughter. I was done taking a beating. I had a little one who was counting on me to be strong. I'd forget about Griffin for the moment and focus on her.

I pulled out my cellphone, dialed my mother's number.

"It didn't work out, but I'm coming home. We'll be ok, Mom." I truly felt that I'd be fine with the baby. And with confidence that I didn't need to fake, I said, "I'm scared, but I know I can do this on my own."

# PART 3

My Happy Ending

"Sadie, don't touch that. Sadie, I'm only going to tell you one more time… do not—"

I lunged forward as she squealed in delight knowing that she beat me to the punch. The screen on my laptop went dark and I realized that hours of work were now probably gone.

I narrowed my eyes at her and shook my finger. She grabbed it and started giggling. I tried to keep my expression stern, but there was no use. Her big smile and dimpled cheeks were too much. She was adorable even when she was harassing me.

I swooped her up to tickle her. Her giggles turned into deep belly laughs. Her laughs were infectious and I found myself laughing too until I was out of breath.

I looked at her smiling face and recalled how much she smiled even as a baby. It was hard to believe that she was almost four now. Her unruly curls stuck up around her head and she looked as if she had been zapped by lightning. She hated for me to do her hair and I learned early as a mom that I needed to pick my battles so unless we were going somewhere in public, she spent her time looking like a little wild child, as my mom would say.

"Ok, Mommy has to work. Go see if Grandma is outside."

She did as I said, which was pretty rare, and ran towards the back door that led to our modest backyard. I knew my mom was back there reading a book on the porch.

I could hear Sadie's voice as she questioned my mom about what she was reading.

"I'm reading a book."

"A big book?"

"Yep."

"With dinosaurs and monsters?" I heard Sadie ask excitedly.

I'm not sure how my mom answered but apparently it tickled Sadie who began to laugh.

She was such a happy kid I thought to myself. I remembered how hard it had been in the beginning. But her sheer happiness had given me a happiness of my own. She had truly been a ray of sunshine. Instead of coming home exhausted every night from school, seeing her had energized me and motivated me, especially when times were tough and loneliness was my best friend.

I'd started going to school again when she was about three months old, studying coding and web development. Since I preferred the idea of keeping Sadie at home over sending her to a pre-school, I knew I needed a job where I could set my own work hours and have plenty of flexibility to raise her. I did some research and then dove headfirst taking classes on the weekends and evenings, even signing up for online classes.

And to my surprise, as soon as I was done I landed a job. Two years on, I moved out of my parents' home and settled into a little rental house a few miles away.

I knew having a baby meant I had to be practical and I knew my career as an actress in small-town Georgia wouldn't exactly help pay the bills, so I did focus on going back to school, but I never stopped acting. It was a stress reliever for me. I starred in several plays put on at the local theater. One had actually gone viral, and I'd been pretty proud. But besides working in web development, I starred in little commercials for a few bigger businesses, mostly furniture places in the area. I'd visited Atlanta a few times to do some modeling work, but not much had come from it except for a few extra thousand dollars every now and then.

I was stunned when I received a casting call from a company in L.A. After a few Skype interviews, I landed a role that would make me and Sadie comfortable for some time.

It had been a month since I'd agreed to the assignment. I was going to play the role of a confused girl in an insurance company ad. I was going alone to L.A. The assignment was only going to be for two weeks tops. I was leaving Sadie behind which was something I'd never done before. In fact, I hadn't spent a night away from her since she was born. The mere thought made me sad, but she adored her grandparents and I knew she'd be well taken care of.

I was leaving in the morning so I'd packed her bag and decided to have a taxi pick me up instead of having Mom drive me. Her sight wasn't as good as it used to be and she tired quickly. My dad was at some sort of convention, so he couldn't do it. But he'd told me to Skype him as soon as I got settled at Kenny's place.

I checked in online and then tied up a few loose ends at work. I was sending an email to a prospective client, letting her know that I'd get back to her in a few weeks. She was a long-time client so she was flexible and always willing to work with me.

As I finished up the email, I heard my mom telling Sadie to come inside. Sadie, of course, whined and tried to convince my mother to let her stay outside with the bugs, but Mom won that fight. Sadie came in pouting and I placed my hands on my hips and gave her a stern look.

"What's with the sad face, young lady?"

She angrily said, "Granny won't let me stay outside."

"Well, do you want to live outside?"

"Yes."

"Are you sure? There's no ice cream outside. If you live outside then how are you going to get ice cream?"

She thought about it long and hard and then she said, "Ok. I'll live here."

I laughed and picked her up. My mom reached for her and said, "Go ahead and finish up your work stuff. I'll get her into a bath and then to bed."

I kissed Sadie on the forehead and she hugged my neck. "Love you, Mommy," she said, burying her head in the crook of my neck. The next two weeks were going to be painful. God, how I was going to miss her.

I passed her over to my mom and blew her a kiss. "I'll see you in a little bit, sweetheart."

She smiled at me and waved goodbye as my mom walked down the hallway into the bathroom with Sadie in her arms. She was tall for her age. Mom told me that at Sadie's age, I'd just been… well… round.

I turned back to work, responding to emails and finishing up some tasks on my own web page that I was revamping.

About half an hour later, I made my way to Sadie's

room. Sadie had helped me paint it with every color of the rainbow. She had a rainbow that she'd made during story time at the library that hung above her vibrant green headboard. Stars of various shapes and colors hung from the ceiling. It had been quite an art project to say the least.

The lights were low so the little stars attached to the ceiling began to glow courtesy of the glow in the dark spray paint we had used to create them.

"How's my little monster?" I asked, pinching her nose playfully.

She swatted at my hand and giggled. "I'm not a monster."

"Oh really?" I said, tickling her and then roaring like a lion. She couldn't stop giggling and I heard my mom laughing from the doorway.

"You two are silly," she said.

"Mommy is super silly!" Sadie yelled.

I nodded. "I sure am." I tucked the sheet around her and thanked my lucky stars that she wasn't going to fight me about going to bed tonight. I figured it was because her granny was here. Sadie was always on her best behavior when her granny and grandpa were around.

I found her favorite stuffed animal, a duck-billed dinosaur that I couldn't readily identify, and stuck it next to her. She promptly wrapped her arms around it and began to snore.

"Well then," I whispered, hoping not to wake her. I bent down and kissed her forehead. I sat there next to her bed for a moment watching her sleep, when I felt my mom's hand on my shoulder.

"She'll be fine, Sunshine. Trust me."

Sunshine was her childhood nickname for me and every now and then she still used it. She said I'd been like a ball of sunshine lighting up her days. I could relate. It was exactly how I felt about Sadie.

We slowly crept out of her room and I left the door slightly ajar, in case she woke up and needed me.

I sat down at the small dining room table and sighed.

"I can't believe I'm saying this, but I feel so guilty leaving her. Not that you're not capable of taking care of her, Mom—"

She raised a brow. "I think she'll be ok. You know, I do have some experience with kids."

I smiled, catching her meaning. "I know she'll be fine, I'll just really miss her."

Mom nodded. "I get it. It was hard for me to go back to work after I had you. If it weren't for the fact bills needed to be paid, I would probably have quit."

"That would have been a terrible decision. You're the best doctor this town has ever had."

She smiled proudly. "I know."

I laughed. My mother had always been confident.

Never arrogant, but self-assured. She always seemed to have everything under control and she never lost her cool. I think that's what made her such a good doctor, she was confident in her skills and cool under pressure, pretty much how she'd been as a mother.

She always made me feel safe and protected. She was always patient with me, even when I was at my worst. I only hoped I would be half the mother she was.

"So, are you excited about the role? I know it's not Hollywood, but who knows, maybe some agent will see you and say to himself, 'That one there! We have to hire her! We just have to!'" she said, imitating a newscaster voice which made me laugh.

"Did you just try to sound like an anchorwoman?"

She shrugged. "Those are the only actresses I'm familiar with."

"They're not actors, Mom."

"Maybe not by profession, but they pretty much are. They get all dressed up, sit stiffly, and pretend to care about everything they're saying."

"Not another tirade about the news…" I whined.

"Ok, I'm done. You sound just like Sadie. I can't believe whining is genetic."

We laughed and then her expression suddenly changed and she sat back in her chair. "So, what's the plan?"

"The plan? To do a great commercial and hope that it leads to more work."

"Not that plan, Nina. You know what I'm talking about." She folded her arms across her chest.

"You're talking about Sadie's father," I said with a sigh. I never said his name. Calling him "Sadie's father" somehow made the relationship seem more clinical… almost as if he were a sperm donor, some anonymous guy, rather than the one who had pretty much ruined me for other men.

"I honestly don't think there's anything that I should do."

"Really?"

"I told you what happened when I tried to talk to him."

"And you just gave up trying," my mom said with disapproval.

"I told you what I saw, who I saw him with. He has a family, Mom. I'm a homewrecker."

"You should have confronted him," she said angrily. I remembered when I had told her everything that happened. She had immediately started crying and then her tears turned into rage and she was ready to fly out to L.A. to defend me. I had to have multiple conversations with my dad to ensure he wouldn't let her get on a plane.

When I'd flown back to Georgia and had seen her

face, I'd started crying all over again as she held me in the airport, rocking me as if I were a baby again.

I felt like a little girl now as she stared at me waiting for me to answer.

I shrugged. "Mom, we've been over this a million times. He has a family. He lied to me. Well, at the very least, he lied by omission. And to be honest, I don't think his crazy mother would take kindly to me calling him again."

"That old hag can go screw herself," my mom growled, catching me off-guard.

"You okay, Mom?" Her words were pretty uncharacteristic of my mild-mannered mother.

"I'm fine. I'm just so mad for you… how humiliating! She had you escorted out like you were a peasant being kicked out of the king's castle. Just because she has money doesn't mean she can treat you like that."

I reached out and placed my hand over hers. "Don't get yourself worked up. It was years ago."

She sighed and placed her face in her hands and took a deep breath before looking up at me with a small smile.

"I just get crazy when I think of anyone harming you, especially if that harm is emotional."

"I get it… I mean, I didn't really before. I thought you were overprotective and overbearing when I was a teenager."

"Thanks, Nina," she said, before becoming serious again. "I think since you're going to L.A. you should at least try to contact him again. You never got to know your father and I—"

"That's not your fault," I said, knowing that my father died when my mother was pregnant with me.

"No, it's not, I know that. But as your aunt so eloquently put it, you hadn't exactly been planned, but I wish I'd told him. He died never knowing."

She looked ready to tear up and I reached for her hand again and squeezed it. "Look at me." She looked up at me with tear-filled eyes. "You didn't know he was going to be deployed."

"Oh," she said, "he wasn't in the military."

"What?"

"I just made that up so that you would have an inter-esting story to tell the kids at school."

"Mom!"

"What?"

"Are you freaking kidding me?"

"Watch your tone, young lady. What was I supposed to tell you? That he died when he went skiing for the first time and ran into a tree?"

I opened my mouth and then closed it. "Really?"

"Yes. He wasn't the most graceful fellow. It's amazing he could even cross the street without getting hit by a bus."

"No wonder you were never interested in skiing."

"Well, that and because I just don't get winter sports. Who wants to be cold, outdoors and exercising? It's nonsensical to me."

"Mom?" I said tiredly, not allowing myself to focus on the fact my mother let me believe a lie she made up for years. I couldn't even be angry with her. I'd always felt the whole military excuse had been a bit too convenient.

"Yes?"

"I'm going to bed." I stood up before she could say another word. I kissed her forehead and then headed for my bedroom wondering if when I closed my eyes that night I'd dream of a certain man.

* * *

"NINA," the director said. "You were great out there. There was so much passion... so much force. I loved every bit of it except the beginning." He gave me a sad look. "And maybe a little bit of the end, the middle was good though."

The makeup artist was fixing my lipstick so I couldn't immediately respond. Once she was done, I thanked her and turned my attention to Jacob Fox, the director. He was a skinny guy. He was probably about 5'8 and weighed 130 pounds. Even though he was very skinny, he had a gut that fell over the waistband of his pants. He wore large glasses and had a deep Texas accent.

I only had three lines, so I wasn't sure what "middle" he was talking about. I could only guess it was the actual part of the script where I had lines and wasn't just sitting there with a stale beer in my hand pretending to be an irresponsible motorist which is what my role really required.

"Ok… what would you like me to do differently?" I said trying to be diplomatic, even though I wanted to ask him what the heck he was talking about.

"I just don't think you fully understand your character's motivation," he said, raising his hands up and artistically making gestures as if I could see whatever he envisioned in his head. "You see, your character is upset, sad, so sad… her new car was just ruined. I need you to give me grief. Come on, Nina, give me your best sorrowful, "woe is me" face."

He stared at me, not speaking.

"Oh, you mean, now?" I asked.

"Uhh, yeah…"

I did as I was told, hoping it would be good enough.

He shook his head in disappointment. "You don't look sad, you look melancholic. There's a difference, you know."

I was spared any more tips about the difference

between sad and melancholic when someone came up and started asking him questions that were apparently a lot more important than lecturing me about the emotions my character should display.

"Don't pay Fox any mind. He doesn't know how to treat a lady."

All the hairs on the back of my neck stood up. I knew that voice… I'd been escorted from a building just to hear it.

"So, let me get this right, you're saying that you do know how to treat a lady?" I said turning around and facing Griffin.

He shrugged. "I try my best."

He leaned against the wall with his arms folded across his chest. I couldn't help but study him. After all, it had been years since I laid eyes on him.

Apparently, he planned to do the same. He was completely clean-shaven with a short military cut on top. It was a different look, and he was rocking it… but I didn't plan to tell him that.

We stood there in silence checking each other out. Not that he'd be impressed by anything I had on. I didn't exactly look "hot." I was wearing plain jeans and a heavy sweater, although it was at least 85 degrees outside today. We were filming a winter scene and between the lights and my wardrobe, I was burning up. My body told me I was burning up for another reason but I didn't dwell on it. I wasn't some starry-eyed, horny 22-year old anymore. Things had changed. I had changed.

And I realized with my new-found confidence that I wasn't scared of facing Griffin anymore.

"You're looking great," he said, giving me a warm, but cautious smile.

I ignored it. "I know. Anyway, I got to get back to work. Nice seeing you again."

I walked away from him feeling powerful. For once, I truly felt that when Griffin was concerned I had the upper hand. But of course, he didn't give up that easily.

He fell into stride next to me. "So, you aren't happy to see me? What's it been? Three? Four years?"

I rolled my eyes. So, he was going to play dumb, huh? Pretend the whole escorting me out of the office with the help of security didn't happen.

"How's your mother?" I spit out.

He looked at me curiously. "Fine. Why do you ask?"

I stopped dead in my tracks and stood chest to chest with him, albeit I was several inches shorter.

"Let's not play games, Griffin. We all know that I showed up nearly four years ago to see you and you didn't see me."

"I was told that you left abruptly. When I came out to get you, you had already left."

I couldn't believe my ears. "Left abruptly? I was escorted out by your security guards."

"What?" he said, clearly taken aback.

I narrowed my eyes. I could remember the events of that office visit like it was yesterday, and I found it hard to believe that he didn't know anything about me being kicked out by his security guards after all these years.

But as I looked in his eyes, I saw no guile there.

"You really don't know what happened at your office when I came to speak with you?"

He opened his mouth to answer when someone hustled over to me and started pulling me to the set. "We need you, now. Come on, let's make it rain for this lame insurance company."

I let her pull me away, but I glanced back at Griffin. I wondered exactly what else he didn't know. If he didn't know that I was escorted out by security, he probably also didn't know that I had arranged to meet him later on. I'd always suspected and knew deep down that Mrs. Wallace had made sure Griffin had never met with me, but that still didn't explain how he could have sex with me when he was a married man with a family.

I pushed away my burgeoning curiosity and instead focused on looking sad, but not melancholy, for the camera.

Hours later I made my way to a bar with a few other people from the set. I honestly didn't know what they all did, but most of them were friendly and seemed like a pretty decent crowd. I was staying with my cousin Kenny again, but I didn't think he'd want to spend all his free time entertaining me, so I figured I might as well make some friends and I also wanted dirt on Griffin. Just exactly what was he doing there? Why was he hanging out on the set of an insurance commercial? From what I could gather from my recent internet stalking, he was into artificial intelligence and had added to his family's fortune that way. He wasn't into insurance or commercials. I didn't know all the details, but from what I could tell, his money came from advancements in technology. Silicon Valley was more his scene, not L.A. No wonder his mom had an extra $250,000 hanging around.

I found the rest of the group and sat down. A handsome young man with dimples that reminded me of Sadie's offered me a seat. I tried my best to remember his name. It was something with a J. Jeremy? Jason? Johnny?

Jerry! That was his name. I think he was a production assistant or an intern. I smiled brightly at him, and he offered me a drink.

"Thanks, Jerry," I said as he handed me a beer. I took a long sip, forgetting how much I liked a nice cold beer.

I barely drank at all since having Sadie. I'd never been a big drinker, but given how I was her main caretaker, I liked to be sure I was fully capable of taking care of her at all times, so I rarely drank except for the occasional spritzer at my mom's house during the holidays.

A few other people joined us and we sat cracking jokes and enjoying good company. The bar was kind of on the dingy side, but had a pretty hip vibe with all the cool global items that adorned the walls.

"So, Nina, I thought I detected a southern accent?" said Jerry as he sat across from me. He was cute. I would guess he was barely 20 though, and he had an adorable baby face. Definitely not my type. Too pretty.

"Yep. Georgia."

"Born and raised?"

"Yep," I said, "What about you?" I said feeling relaxed. Raising Sadie was a full-time commitment, and other than speaking to my parents I didn't get much adult conversation. Even if Jerry was years younger than me, it was definitely nice to relax and have a laid-back conversation with a peer.

"Grew up in Rahway, New Jersey, and have no intention of going back. It's easily the most depressing place on Earth."

"That's harsh."

"So was life in Rahway," he joked. "Dark, gray, miserable." He playfully shuddered and smiled at me.

I smiled back. I had a feeling that Jerry was flirting with me. I felt a little bad that I wasn't even remotely attracted to him. He was a nice guy, I could tell, but not the type I dated. Not that I dated much anymore. I actually hadn't had a date since before I met Griffin. I internally winced…

What was I doing with my life? Oh yeah, raising a beautiful little girl.

Thinking about her, I realized that I was a few minutes late of my scheduled call home.

"Excuse me, Jerry. I'll be right back. I just have to make a quick call." I hoped he didn't assume I had faked a call to try to get away from him. I didn't want to hurt the poor guy's feelings. But it was just as well, I'd have to break it to him anyway that not only wasn't I interested, but that I lived states away and had no intention of sticking around in L.A.

I got up and made my way to the outside of the bar and dialed my mother's number. She picked it up immediately.

"Hi!" she said happily. And then quickly came the questions. "Did you Skype your dad? He's worried about you."

"Ughh," I said popping my forehead with the heel of my hand. I totally forgot.

"He's going to be so worried."

I already felt guilty enough about forgetting. "Don't

worry, I'll call him. Is Sadie sleeping? If so, don't wake her. Sorry for my late call, I got distracted here by… things."

"No, she's not sleeping. Let me get her. Do you want to see her? I can do a video call…"

"Yes, please."

Excited about seeing her little face, I could barely stop smiling from ear to ear. I know it had been less than a day but I missed her the moment I left her behind.

She had been my everything and had kept me from succumbing to my own stupid emotions, which alternated between animosity and hatred towards Griffin.

"Hi! Mommy!" she said again with a giggle.

"What's so funny?" I asked giving her my best impression of one of her favorite cartoon characters.

She giggled even more.

Finally, my mom stepped in and said, "Tell her what you did today."

"I ate chicken nuggets. I played. I want to watch TV."

"Of course, you do," I said with a smile. "But can't you talk a little bit more to your mom here? I've missed you so." I made an exaggerated sad face, which made her giggle.

"I miss you too, Mommy!" Sadie said.

We spoke for a little while longer and then I ended the call. Right on time it seemed as I looked up and found Griffin heading towards the bar. Who had invited him?

"Care for some company?" he asked, holding the door open for me. I muttered a thank you and quickly rushed past him. I didn't want to get too close to him. His presence was unnerving, so much so that I found myself still talking.

"I have plenty of company. Jerry, for example." I was surprised by my own comment. Was I subconsciously trying to make Griffin jealous?

He scoffed. "Jerry? He's barely out of his teens and he's hitting on you?"

Mission accomplished. Apparently, he was jealous.

"What makes you think I mind?" I was deliberately baiting him. His presence annoyed me and reminded me why I had to be careful about who I trusted. I wasn't that naïve little girl anymore. I was a mother. Sadie's mother. My Sadie was Griffin's daughter. I tried not to think about the secret I was keeping from him as he seated himself directly next to me.

You could see the mood around the table change when Griffin sat down. I'm pretty sure he hadn't been invited.

Jerry looked at him as if he was fly in his soup and took his attention away from me to talk to the pretty waitress who was coming around to take our orders. I sighed. Griffin was great at ruining things for me. I tried to jump into other conversations going on around the table, but that wasn't very successful. The crowd was much more sedated now that an outsider was around. And why exactly was he there?

I tried in vain to inject myself into a conversation with Jerry, but he was now on his cellphone texting or doing whatever.

Griffin waved a hand in my face, as if to get my attention, and I slapped at it and glared at him.

"What? I was just trying to see if I were invisible to you suddenly."

I ignored him and took a sip of my drink.

He shrugged. "Funny, I remember you being a lot more fun before."

I gave him an evil look before saying, "Funny, I don't remember the same about you."

He laughed. "So what have you been up to all these years?"

"That's my business."

"So, secretive… no sense of humor… You've changed over the years."

"You have no idea," I said cryptically, looking for a polite way to end the evening and get the hell out of there. I didn't like this at all. The last thing I wanted to do was sit around and chitchat with Griffin as if the past four years hadn't happened. And to be honest, his nearness was bothering me.

I decided to just be blunt, a skill I'd learned to get out of all sorts of mommy expectations like carpools and playdates. Being a single mom, I didn't have the luxury of blaming a spouse when I wanted to get out of things, so I'd learned to be direct instead.

"I'm heading out. See you guys later."

"So soon?" Jerry said, standing up too. "Hey, let me give you a ride." I had a sneaky suspicion that he was trying to wait out Griffin. I think his plan had been to ignore Griffin until he eventually left and then talk to me.

"She already has a ride," Griffin said before I could speak.

"I'll see you tomorrow, Jerry," I said, ignoring Griffin and making my way towards the exit again. Of course, Griffin fell into step next to me.

I ignored him and headed towards a bus stop.

"Jerry seems to have a crush on you."

I shrugged and sat down on the bench. He surprised me by sitting down next to me.

"This is a first, a billionaire sitting down at a bus stop."

"I've caught my share of buses."

"Really? When and where?"

He smiled. "Well, I could have if I wanted to. So why are you avoiding me?"

"I'm not avoiding you. I just have nothing to say to you."

"Listen, I know things didn't end well for us on the island..."

"That's one way to put it," I mumbled.

"And I had no idea that security had you escorted out when you dropped by the office. I knew you'd stopped by, but I had to take a call and my receptionist said you'd left abruptly. There must have been a misunderstanding."

I scoffed. "I was thrown out by security, I didn't leave abruptly."

"Again, I'm sorry. I have no idea how that happened or why I didn't know anything about it."

I looked at him then, really looked at him. He met my eyes straight on and I knew he wasn't lying to me. As I'd expected, his mother clearly had been behind the debacle that day in the office. But that didn't explain what I'd seen that day on the beach. The anger towards him that I thought I'd buried years ago raised its ugly head.

"Got it. You're pleading ignorance. Fine. Now go away."

"Come on, Nina. You're not the type to hold a grudge."

I shot him a look and raised my brows. "Don't go

there. You don't know anything about me, so don't pretend that you do."

He seemed taken aback by my hostility towards him. Good, I thought.

"Maybe. But I'd like the opportunity to get to know you... again. We met when I had a lot going on and I'm sorry that I didn't follow up—"

"You had a lot going on! Care to share with me exactly what?" I challenged him.

He hesitated as if trying to decide how much to tell me, and my eyes narrowed. "Stop wasting my time, Griffin."

"If I didn't know any better, I'd say that you hate me."

"Hate you? I don't even think about you." I was lying. I thought about him all the time. And that was the problem. Despite my cold demeanor, I'd spent years fantasizing that what I saw hadn't been his real family, that there had been some sort of mistake. I'd never admit the time I spent searching for information about him and his family on the internet and how I got nowhere. He and his family stayed out of the public eye. At the very least, they weren't socialites.

"If you don't hate me then I guess you wouldn't mind joining me for dinner tomorrow night?"

"I'm busy."

"How about this weekend then?"

"No."

"Ok, how about lunch then?"

"No thanks."

"Come on, you have to eat. You might as well share a meal with me."

My phone started ringing and I reached for it, becoming anxious when I realized that it was my mom. I stood up and walked away from him, not bothering to excuse myself. I walked out of hearing distance, not wanting to be overheard. "Mom, is everything okay with Sadie?"

"Oh yes, everything's fine. Sorry to scare you. I just noticed that she has a little cough and I was wondering if you think it's a good idea to take her to that preschool story time at the library."

"She has a cough?" I asked, concerned.

"Just a cold, nothing to worry about."

I breathed out in relief, not realizing that I'd been holding my breath. "Yeah, skip the library. I would hate if Patrick or any of her other little friends caught anything from her."

"Ok. So have you decided whether or not you're going to talk to her father?" That came out of nowhere and I rolled my eyes. I should have expected *this* call.

"Aha! The real reason for this call. We'll discuss this later, Mom."

"But, Nina—"

"Good night, Mom. I'm hanging up now."

I found Griffin standing up, leaning against the bus stop staring at me with his arms folded.

"Still taking calls from your mother..." I knew he was teasing me, but I was pretty immune to his flirtatious teasing now.

"You're one to talk," I shot back.

"What's that supposed to mean?"

"Come on, Griffin," I said angrily. "And don't you have family that you should be checking up on instead of hanging out with a random woman at a bus stop in the middle of the night?"

He looked at me curiously. I didn't wait for him to answer as I saw Jerry walking out of the restaurant.

"Hey, Jerry!" I called, "Can I still get that ride?"

Jerry looked at me in surprise and then looked at Griffin.

He gave a boyish shrug, though his tone was clearly unsure as he said, "Uhh yeah... sure."

Without a backward glance, I walked away from Griffin. And I hoped this time it was forever.

## 7

"It's creepy how you just pop up on set uninvited," I said to Griffin as he handed me a cup of coffee. It was the next day and I was feeling a little drowsy. I hadn't gotten much sleep that night. I'd spent most of the night tossing and turning, wondering if I should tell Griffin about Sadie now I had the opportunity.

Part of me felt guilty for not telling him and then I reminded myself that he never gave me the opportunity. Well, his mother never did. But from what it seemed, we were both keeping secrets... at least I had attempted to tell him mine all those years ago. He hadn't shown me the same courtesy. So as far as I was concerned, Griffin was still the enemy.

"I'm a friend of the director," he explained. I doubted that was true.

"Of course you are…"

"You don't believe me?"

"Sorry if I don't find you exactly truthful."

"I'm not sure why. I've never lied to you…"

The nerve! It took all my self-control not to scream at him or toss my coffee at him.

"You've never lied to me? Seriously?"

He put both his hands up as if warding me off. "Woah. Stop aiming that coffee at me. And what makes you think I lied to you?"

I sat the coffee down, placed my hands on my hips and was ready to tell him exactly what I saw all those years ago when out of nowhere Jerry appeared.

"Hi, Griffin." He stood between us and kept his back turned to Griffin as he greeted me. "Hey, Nina… I just wanted to double check that we're still on for this weekend?"

"What?" I was clueless as to what he was talking about. And then I remembered briefly about some sporting event he had asked me to… ultimate frisbee or something. I had at the time thought it would be harmless so I'd agreed. Now I was regretting it. Jerry was nice, but I had other problems, like the one standing behind Jerry who was glaring at both of us.

"I'll be there," I chirped, wanting to make Griffin angrier and not caring that it was just a frisbee game…I had no problem letting him think it was something more serious.

"Great!" Jerry said, placing a hand up and I awkwardly high-fived him. I couldn't help but smile. He was so cute. He was smart enough to not say anything else to Griffin who stood there looking ready to hit him.

"Calm down," I said, a small smile on my face as Jerry walked away. I was enjoying this.

"So, you can go to dinner with him but not me?"

"Sure looks that way." I deliberately kept my voice nonchalant.

"What do you see in that kid?" He scoffed. "Is he even old enough to drink?"

"Stop being jealous, it's not a good look on you."

He placed his hand on his chin as if pensive and said teasingly, "Maybe I can get Jerry reassigned."

"You wouldn't!"

"Yes, I would."

"How do you even have the authority to do that?"

"I know the casting director... Richard."

I looked at him inquisitively, "Richard? Richard Hayes is the casting director? I didn't know. I only met with an assistant each time. He's the guy who hired me to work at the resort."

"Yeah, Richard's my cousin."

"Small world," I said, now finally understanding why Richard had known exactly where Griffin would be all those years ago. It also explained why Griffin always spoke about Richard as if he knew him very well. I don't know why I didn't figure this out before.

And suddenly another piece of the puzzle fell into place. I bet Mrs. Wallace had insisted on coming to the auditions to ensure Richard only picked women she approved of to be around her sons. I had clearly been a last-minute addition, a wild card.

"I wouldn't figure Richard would be related to you."

"Well, he looks a lot different from me, but—"

"No," I said looking him squarely in the eye. "He's a decent person, which is more than I can say for you."

I walked away, not giving him a chance to answer and went to my place on set. He didn't leave, he just watched me. Any time he tried to approach me during a break I made sure I was busy talking to someone else, especially Jerry. By the end of the day, I was feeling quite accomplished and I was thoroughly enjoying making Griffin jealous.

He finally caught up with me about six hours into production when I was in makeup again.

"Hey," he said to the makeup artist, giving her a charming smile that brought back memories I'd rather forget. "Do you mind giving us some privacy for a second?"

She looked at me and then up at Griffin and shrugged. "Two minutes. I need to do a few touch-ups."

I sighed as I sat up in my chair. "Griffin. Don't you work? Don't you have a corporation to run? Why are you hanging out here like a sad puppy?"

"I'm not a sad puppy. I'm an alpha wolf. Remember that."

I spun around in my chair and gave him a long look. "Ever since you overheard my conversation with Jerry, or rather, eavesdropped on my conversation with Jerry, you've looked like a sad puppy. A sad Great Dane puppy."

He perked up. "At least Great Danes are feared and respected dogs."

"I was thinking more along the lines of Scooby-Doo."

"Ouch, now that was low."

"I shouldn't have insulted Scooby like that. After all, Scooby doesn't have an issue with his moral compass."

"What's that supposed to mean?" He narrowed his eyes at me.

I looked down at his hand meaningfully, not seeing a ring there.

"How's the missus doing? How's your kid?" My tone was even, light even as if what I found out all those years ago didn't matter, as if I hadn't been unforgivably hurt by him.

He gave me a puzzled look and was about to say something when the makeup artist reappeared. "Time's up," she said, unceremoniously pushing me back into the chair.

"What makes you think I'm married?" he asked, standing on the opposite side of the makeup artist.

I was shocked that he wanted to have that conversation right here and now within listening distance of a complete stranger.

"Lower your voice," I hissed. "I'm working, in case you haven't noticed."

The makeup artist sighed as if she wanted to be anywhere else but around us and I instantly felt bad.

"Sorry," I said to her.

She shrugged. "This isn't the worst I've heard by far. People think bartenders and stylists have to hear more than they want. Ha! They should try being a makeup artist. It really sheds light on how much people suck!" And with that she walked away, leaving me alone with Griffin again.

"Explain."

"I don't have to explain anything to you, Griffin. Quit acting dumb," I said and my Southern accent deepened as I became upset.

"I have no clue what you're talking about... I'm not married."

"Maybe you aren't married now but all the evidence supports that you were married then."

"What evidence?" he said crossing his arms over his

chest. He was wearing a plain white t-shirt and jeans and jeez he looked good. I tried not to notice that as I responded.

"Let's see... you sleep with me and then randomly leave the island and when I do try to contact you again, I'm escorted out by security."

"That was all a misunderstanding."

"Really? Your mother didn't seem to think so."

"My mother? You've met my mother?"

"Unfortunately, I've had several run-ins with your mother!"

"What?"

I shook my head. He really had no clue about what was going on outside his own little world. That realization just served to piss me off even more.

"Listen, I don't know what's going on here, but I need some answers. And I don't know how my mom's involved in all this, or why she's involved in all this." He placed his hands on his hips and stared past me in deep thought. "I need to get some answers." He turned away from me and walked away, leaving me staring after him.

"Miss Charles! We're ready for you!" called the production assistant and I hurriedly made my way to set wondering what answers Griffin might find.

To my surprise, there was no sign of Griffin for a few days after our confrontation. I didn't know what to think about that. My feelings, whenever Griffin was concerned, were always conflicted. I thought about him as I sat on the couch eating fancy cupcakes with Kenny on the edge of the couch watching me.

"Girl, like really, girl... you haven't stopped eating since you got here. Can you slow down? You do want to fit on the plane when you head back to Georgia, right?"

I punched him in his thigh. He was wearing really short shorts so my punch actually hit skin.

"Ouch," he said giving me a hurt look. He was lanky and wasn't very muscular, so maybe my half-hearted punch had hurt a little. "I'm just worried about your blood sugar level," he complained. "You've eaten two pints of ice cream and four cupcakes and it's only been one hour."

"I'm depressed."

He sighed. "Honey, you shouldn't eat your emotions. You beat them up instead. Come on. I have to sub a kickboxing class. You'll love it. You can beat your emotions away or pretend to be beating up a certain someone who shall remain nameless."

He knew all about Griffin and had volunteered to have his car booted. Kenny liked to think he knew people in high places.

I felt like throwing up suddenly. I'd had one cupcake

too many. He was right. I put the cupcake down and said, "Alright, let's do this."

We rode in Kenny's car and on the way there I filled him in on my most recent encounters with Griffin.

"Oh, my God, so he's just playing stupid. You can't trust them. You just can't trust men, Nina!" He said hitting the steering wheel really hard.

I gave him a long look. "Having trouble with Cyril?" I hadn't seen Cyril since I'd arrived, but I'd been so wrapped up in my own problems, I hadn't asked Kenny about what was going on.

"Trouble... girl, you don't know trouble," he growled.

"Alright tell me everything. What's going on?"

"He wants to move. He wants to leave L.A. and go live somewhere in nowhere Texas and own a winery."

"What? There are wineries in Texas?"

"Exactly! That's what I said!"

"Why would he want to do that?"

"Nina, I don't know. Apparently, he's lost his mind. He doesn't even drink wine! How can he own a winery?"

"So, is that why he's not around?"

"Yeah, he's looking at property."

He pulled up to the gym and took out his cellphone. He started scrolling through photos that Cyril had recently sent him. Most of them were of Cyril wearing cowboy hats, standing in rows of vines. It was actually really pretty, completely unexpected. I hadn't visited

Texas before and part of me just assumed it was mostly flat land and desert. The pictures proved me wrong.

"Apparently, Texas is a well-known wine-producing state," Kenny mumbled angrily.

"But why Texas? Why not open a winery here in California?"

"California's too expensive. I don't know what's gotten into him. He started taking sommelier classes and now he thinks it's his life's calling to grow grapes." The way to described it made it sound especially absurd.

"Not to be nosey, but how is he going to pay for a winery? I'm guessing even a cheap one is expensive."

"Trust fund."

"Jeez, is everyone in L.A. rich but me?"

"Some days it seems like it."

I couldn't help but laugh. We got out of the car and entered a weird looking metal building. It looked like an airport hangar in a Salvador Dali painting. The inside of the gym didn't have a floor. There were a bunch of little rocks under our feet with large abstract sculptures artfully displayed a few feet from each other.

"This is different," I remarked.

"I know. Isn't it cool?"

I smiled tightly. Cool definitely wasn't the word I would use, but I didn't want to say anything that would offend Kenny. Clearly, this was unlike any gym I had seen before.

After we passed the rock garden, we entered a lounge with a concrete floor. The lounge was very minimalist with just a single steel bench in front of a large metal desk. Sitting behind the desk was a beautiful bald woman wearing a long flowing robe. She smiled at Kenny, who blew her a kiss. I followed him into a studio area.

Finally, something that actually looks like a gym, I said to myself. There were about 20 large punching bags in the room and the attendees stood around quietly wrapping their hands with long pieces of fabric or stretching, doing weird splits on the floor. Boxing gloves were scattered across the room, others were resting on top of the punching bags or near the wall.

Kenny waved hello to everyone and then went to a locker and handed me a pair of gloves.

"Pick a bag, hon."

I did as I was told and then I stood awkwardly with my gloves in my hand and then started to put them on when the other girls did too.

"Ladies, this is my cousin, Nina!" he said into the microphone hanging from his ear. "Let's give her a great big welcome!"

"Hi, Nina!" everyone shouted, making me smile.

"Nina here is visiting from Georgia! My old stomping grounds! She's having some man problems..."

I shot Kenny an evil look as he shared my business with the other strangers in the room.

"But don't we all?" he said, laughing and I could hear a snicker or two. I tried to keep from blushing, but I was sure I was turning red.

"Alright ladies, find a partner. Let's do this!" shouted Kenny, and there was a lot of howling and whistling.

I found a partner and tried to keep up with all the jab, cross and uppercut sequences, but my coordination was mediocre at best. My arms got tired as I was practicing with my partner and her jab caught me in the eye, sending me sprawling.

"Uh oh!" Kenny said, running over to me. "Now class, this is an important lesson. This is exactly why we keep our guard up, right?"

"Right," they echoed.

Kenny happily jogged away to continue teaching class and another assistant instructor gave me an ice bag. She was nice and asked me if I wanted to quit, but I wasn't a quitter... usually. As soon as partner drills were over we started what he called bag rounds. I barely made it through to the end of class. When it was over, I collapsed onto the floor, breathing hard, covered in sweat.

Kenny said goodbye to all the students and then leaned over me. I stared up at him.

"Hey, hon. You ok?"

I shook my head. "My body. My poor body. And my eye... my body and my eye. Everything hurts."

"She barely hit you," he said, helping me up.

"Whatever, I'm sure it's going to be puffy and swollen tomorrow."

"You don't know what you're talking about."

"I've been hit by a truck."

"You can tell you're an actress, drama is definitely your specialty."

"You're so catty."

"Meow," he said, wrapping an arm around my shoulder. I leaned on him, grateful that he was taking care of me. I'd missed him when I'd returned to Georgia.

When I started feeling less sore, I also started feeling more charitable. "You're the best cousin in the world. Thank you for getting me off the couch."

"You're welcome... but honestly, I wanted to join in on your junk food binge since I'm so miserable, but I'm just too disciplined to eat crap like that."

"Thanks for that insightful information," I said sarcastically.

He laughed and then instantly his smile faded as he thought about Cyril. "This whole Cyril situation has got me down. I left Georgia for a reason and I have no interest in going back to the same type of situation. I'm pretty sure Texas will be just as welcoming to our kind as Georgia had been."

I knew what he was talking about. As far as I knew, he'd been the only openly gay kid at school. He'd been bullied and picked on. The administration hadn't done much. And so, his mother had sent him to L.A. to live with his father. I'd missed my cousin, but I'd understood.

"The world's changing, Kenny."

"Not fast enough," he said softly.

I looked at him and could see that he was truly upset. Not much got Kenny down, but apparently this situation with Cyril was weighing on him.

"Do you need a hug?"

"I'm not five anymore," he said, and then looked up at me. "But I'll still take a hug."

I embraced him and as I pulled away, I heard someone clear their voice.

I instantly stiffened when I saw her. "Mrs. Wallace."

"I see you're still getting around," she said succinctly. She was wearing designer leggings and a tank top. She looked like she was in great shape. What's that saying? The evil ones are always well preserved. She then walked away from me without uttering another word.

"Woah, that's one cold bi—"

"Kenny!" I admonished him.

"What? I wasn't going to say anything bad."

"Please! We both know that's not true."

He shook his head. "I think she covered me with frost by just glaring at me."

I laughed. "Let's go."

When we were in the car, he said, "I'm sad that you had to deal with the Ice Queen alone. She's no Elsa, that's for sure."

"Kenny," I said, thoughtfully. "Earlier, Griffin said that he wasn't married."

Kenny glanced at me and then back at the road. "But I thought you said that you saw him with his wife and child..."

"That's what I thought I saw, but what if I jumped to conclusions?" I shook my head sadly. "Then that would mean I single-handedly deprived Sadie of years she could have spent getting to know her father."

"I don't know," Kenny said uneasily. "You did what you thought was right. You made the best decision you could based on all the variables around you."

"I know, but—"

"No, buts. You can't go back, so there's no need to worry yourself about the past."

He was right, but when we pulled into our neighborhood I couldn't help but wonder if I had let the scared little Nina win. Was it because of my cowardice my daughter didn't have a father?

I was in a contemplative mood most of the night as I

lay in Kenny's guest bedroom. I felt ridiculous, staying up thinking about Griffin, but I couldn't help myself.

I couldn't deny that this trip to L.A. had me second guessing the decisions I made all those years ago. But Kenny was right, that was all in the past. I needed to focus on making things right in the present. Feeling conflicted, I closed my eyes and drifted off into a restless sleep.

8

———

"So, are you really going to go out with him?" Griffin asked, sitting down next to me while I waited on set.

I sighed heavily. I hadn't slept well that night and it was all his fault. I was naturally angry with him, even if he hadn't done anything directly to cause it.

"What I do in my free time is none of your business, Griffin."

"You know my friends call me Griff."

"You're not my friend."

"I'd like to be…"

I looked at him sharply. The statement caught me off-guard. I stared into his eyes and realized that he meant it.

"Come on, Nina. I'm not a bad guy. You know that."

"Actually, I don't know. We barely know each other."

"We could change that."

He was right, but I didn't want to talk to him. After all, he hadn't answered my question from the other day.

"I know things between us didn't end well. I know in your opinion you don't have a reason to trust me, especially after the way things ended between us on the island. "

"That's one way to put it."

"Listen, join me for dinner. That's all I'm asking for. Nothing more, nothing less."

"Why? Why even bother?" I said mostly to myself.

"Closure?"

"Ha!"

"Ok, maybe because the other day you wanted answers that I couldn't give you. I want to give you those answers."

I considered his words. I needed answers... not just for me but for Sadie.

"Tonight then."

He smiled widely. "I'm glad. I'll see you tonight." He walked away, clearly not interested in the commercial now that he had apparently got what he wanted. I was afraid I'd made it too easy for him.

"I'll send the car for you," he yelled as he sauntered out. I couldn't help but stare at his butt and then his words sunk in.

"What? No! I'll just meet you somewhere!" I yelled back, but it was too late. He was already gone.

"Great, just great," I said shaking my head... what the heck had I just agreed to?

I spent the rest of the day trying to not mess up my lines. I was so distracted. I decided to call Mom and Sadie when I could no longer think straight. I missed home so much. I didn't reach them and looked at the time. I forgot about the time difference and assumed they were probably watching TV together and Mom was away from her phone.

I decided to call Dad instead. I knew he would just be sitting around looking at some genealogy stuff while Mom and Sadie drifted off in front of the TV.

He picked up immediately, like I knew he would.

"So finally, you call your dad... I was beginning to feel like you forgot about us Southern folks down here."

I laughed. "Hi to you too, Daddy. How are you? How's work?"

"Work sucks."

I shook my head. "Tell me how you really feel, Dad."

He laughed softly. "Your mom and Sadie are knocked out on the couch. I guess you tried to call them already?"

"You guessed right."

"I knew it. I'm second picking."

"Hey, second picking is just as good as first."

We chatted for a while until he gave a big yawn. "It's nap time for me."

"Dad, you're so old," I joked.

"Yep. Sure am. And proud of it. Stay safe out in California. We miss you. Don't get tempted into staying, you hear?"

"Yes, Dad."

"Did you talk to Sadie's co-founder?"

I sighed. He was referring to Griffin. "No. I haven't spoken to him yet about Sadie."

"Well, you should. It's important for a little girl to know her father."

"Well, no matter what happens with her co-founder, she always has you."

"Hmm..." he grunted. "I'm old."

"Yet when I say it, you have an issue with it?" I loved teasing him about his age.

"Hey, you know what they say, you never ask a gentleman his age."

"It's actually you never ask a lady her age."

"Maybe you're right."

I laughed and we hung up after I promised to do a better job calling him. After speaking with my dad, I felt better about my plans with Griffin. I didn't tell Dad my plans to meet with Griffin, but I knew he would approve. I thought how funny it was that even when we're older our parents' approval still mattered. I guessed even an adult never stops being someone's baby.

I focused on getting dressed for the evening. I noticed that Griffin hadn't asked my number or where I was staying. Either he stalked me or he went through my HR file. Probably both.

An hour later I was ready and sitting on the couch with Kenny. The doorbell rang and I had to fight with Kenny to get to the door. He dashed in front of me and pushed me back.

"Kenny!" I hissed.

He stuck his tongue out at me and said, "I just want to meet him and I know you didn't plan to introduce me."

"I sure didn't because you're crazy."

He curtsied to me and then opened the door. "Hiii! You must be Griffin!"

Griffin smiled charmingly, not missing a beat. "I sure am. And you're..."

"Her cousin, Kenny."

"Of course... and you own this fine establishment."

"Guilty as charged," Kenny said with a wink.

Griffin gave him a devilish smile that for some reason made me jealous.

"Kenny, don't you have something you need to take care of?" I cut in, ducking under his arm to join Griffin on the other side of the door.

"No."

"Bye, Kenny."

I walked out the door leaving Kenny pouting. "Have fun you two!" he called. "Don't do anything I wouldn't do."

Griffin smiled and tried to wrap an arm around my shoulders. I pushed his arm down.

"Well, this night is getting off to a great start."

"Tell me about it," I growled. "Oh, you're actually driving." For some reason, I had expected to see the Bentley, but instead there was a large luxury SUV sitting in our small parking lot.

"Well, I didn't plan to, but my driver, who you met in the parking garage that time, insisted on spending this evening with his wife celebrating their 20th anniversary."

"How selfish," I joked.

"That's what I told him."

He opened the door for me and tried to help me in. It took all my strength not to hit at his hand.

"Aren't you the perfect gentleman?"

"I try."

"Not hard enough."

"This is going to be a great evening. I can already tell."

I laughed.

I was silent in the car. And grateful for the darkness

and spacious interior. It gave me room away from Griffin and time to think. I didn't have anything I wanted to say that hadn't already been said. I was just waiting for him to speak.

"So, how's your brother?" I asked when I couldn't take the silence much longer.

"Great. He's expecting a baby soon. I think in a month or two."

So, Sadie was going to have a little cousin, I thought to myself.

"That's great. Tell him I said congratulations."

"I will."

We pulled up to a stop sign and he took his hands off the wheel. "I don't even know where to start," he said, turning to me. "So, let me start at the beginning."

"What beginning?"

"The island."

"Yeah, that's a great place to start."

"I left that day on the island because my sister needed me. Well, my niece needed me. I got a call from my niece's nanny. My sister had been gone for a week, no call, no show."

"Did something happen to her?" I was instantly worried, but didn't want to show it. What if this was all a well-orchestrated lie?

He nodded, "Rehab... eventually. She was in the hospital. She's in recovery now."

I shook my head, "So you left to—"

"Go get my niece. I didn't want her sitting in foster care for even a few minutes and I knew once the authorities found out that my sister had abandoned her kid to get drunk and high, that they would remove Rory from my sister's home."

"So, your sister just didn't come back home and checked herself into rehab?"

"Not exactly. We found her in the hospital a few days later. She had overdosed and someone had brought her in as a Jane Doe."

"Oh my gosh, I'm so sorry… How old was your niece at the time?"

"Three."

"She must have been traumatized."

"Her nanny did a great job staying when she wasn't even being paid. She's a good person. And she also happened to be a close friend of mine from college."

That explained the beach scene… I thought to myself. I must have seen him with his niece and her nanny, who was his friend.

Now that I thought about it… Mrs. Wallace had never called the kid Griffin's kid. She'd only referred to the little girl as her granddaughter. She'd been careful not to fully lie to me… she'd just planted the seed. She had played me like a fool as I had initially suspected.

"I thought… I thought you were married. I saw you

on a beach a few years ago with your arms around some woman and you guys had a little girl."

"My dad raised me better than that. I've never cheated on anyone and I've never been married. The only thing I'm guilty of is failing to tell you that I was leaving the night after we made love, but I was operating on not much sleep because of our lovemaking and when I got that call in the middle of the night, I just left. I wasn't thinking straight."

"But as soon as I came back to my senses I told Jackson to tell you I had to leave."

"He tried," I said. "But I jumped to conclusions and didn't listen. I assumed he was lying... you know, trying to cover for you."

And just like that, my world changed. The man I'd pegged the enemy for years was actually a good, decent guy. I sighed. So now instead of anger, I had to deal with guilt.

Thankfully, soon after, we pulled up to the restaurant and I climbed out of the car before he could come around and open the door.

"I guess I need to get faster," he commented wryly. He reached for my hand and I hesitated before letting him take it. He smiled and I looked away, too overwhelmed by what I'd learned to look at him. And the sad part was that the night was still early. What other secrets was Griffin keeping and when would I have to share my own?

We walked into the restaurant and were seated immediately. It was a cozy Italian place and I desperately wanted something rich and decadent to eat. My stomach growled as I smelled all the mesmerizing aromas in the air.

"You'll like this place, it's delicious."

"It sure smells delicious."

"What are you in the mood for?"

"Cheese, pasta, cream, bread… all of it. And maybe cheesecake at the end?"

He laughed. "I think we can make that happen."

He ordered for the both of us and when the waiter left, I felt vulnerable and unsure of myself. It was like being 22 all over again.

"What's wrong?" he asked.

"Nothing, I just haven't done this in a long time."

"What exactly haven't you done in a long time?" he asked not understanding.

"This… the whole dating scene."

"I get it…neither have I. Life's been busy, to say the least. What's your excuse?" he asked turning the tables.

I gulped. Should I tell him now? Was now the right time? Thankfully, the waiter appeared with a bottle of wine. It gave me time to think, which I was having trouble doing when Griffin was around.

"As you were saying," Griffin prompted me, not letting me forget that I had yet to answer his question.

"I've been busy with life, too busy to date."

"Care to elaborate?" he asked perceptively, knowing there was more.

I stared into his eyes, trying to read him. Trying to see if somehow he already knew or had guessed. But his eyes revealed nothing and I figured I was just being paranoid.

"These past years have been busy. I've been busy dealing with everything that life has thrown at me so I haven't had much time for anything else," I answered cryptically.

He nodded. "I understand that. I found myself in a similar situation."

I inwardly sighed in relief, grateful that he was going to leave the subject alone and not pry. But nope, I was wrong.

"Tell me about your life there. What do you do? I can't imagine there are a lot of opportunities for actresses in small town Georgia."

"There aren't but I keep myself busy. I'm a front-end developer."

"You're a computer geek?" he said, smiling proudly at me.

"Sure am. The entry level salary was exactly what I needed at the time and the economic outlook for the career is great."

He laughed at me then. "You sound like a career counselor."

"I had to make money. I have mouths to feed."

"Mouths?" He looked at me curiously.

God, I wanted to kick myself. This is not how I planned to tell him about Sadie. Actually, I don't know how I planned to tell him about Sadie and it was clear that I needed to.

"It's just a Southern figure of speech." I promptly changed the subject. "So, did your mom tell you everything that happened in your office that day?"

He sat back and sighed. He folded his hands in front of him. "She only admitted to having you escorted out. She said she thought you were a stalker, but she emphasized to me that she just felt sorry for you."

"Stalker! Sorry for me! I was scared spitless! I thought she was going to have me arrested and she's making the whole incident sound as if I were some sort of crazed gold digger."

"My mother does have a way of spinning the truth."

"Ha!" I laughed bitterly. "Tell me about it."

"Let's not talk about my mom. I didn't bring you here for that. Let's keep talking about you. I want to know more about your new career."

"Not much to tell. I'm good at it. It pays well like I mentioned and I can work from home." I stopped myself from continuing about how as a mom I needed that flexibility. "Anyway, it allows me flexibility which is what most millennials want, well according to all the stuff I read on career websites."

"I guess your teacher was wrong, after all," he said as he poured me a glass of wine.

I tilted my head in confusion.

He laughed. "I have a great memory," he said with a shrug. "You said on the island that your programming teacher commented that you couldn't apply yourself. Apparently, he or she was wrong."

Knowing that he remembered that piece of information from a conversation we had years ago, made my heart soften towards him even more.

"Yeah, she was wrong. I guess I just needed the right motivation," I said furtively and then immediately regretted my words. Sadie had been that motivation, but my emotions were too raw and the information I'd uncovered was too new for me to want to add a conversation about Sadie to an already emotionally charged evening.

"You didn't give up on your dream to become an actress, did you?"

I shrugged. "It wasn't ever really my dream, I realized that over the years. It was just something to do while I figured out what I wanted in life."

"And did you figure out what that something was?" I

didn't like his tone. Something about it was unnerving. And I realized suddenly that all the anger I felt towards him had dissipated. And I started to feel things towards him that I hadn't allowed myself to feel in years. I still had a thing for my baby's father.

I shrugged. "Not yet. Maybe one day I will," I replied softly. I yawned and looked at the time. It was growing late and I suggested we head back.

"Already tired of me?"

I smiled at him. "I had a great evening… it's just late."

"Maybe we can do this again some time?" he asked hopefully. When I hesitated, he jumped in, saying, "Just think about it. No pressure. Maybe we can start again? Make up for lost time and pick up where we left off."

"I… well... a lot has happened since we met. I've changed. My priorities have changed. Plus, I'm not going to be here for long."

He shrugged. "I can tell Richard to pull a few strings… maybe he can get you another gig."

"I have a life back in Georgia."

"Let's talk about something else." He leaned forward and reached for my hands, taking them in his. His touch sent a chill up my arms and I couldn't think or breathe for a moment.

"Everything you think you know about me is wrong. I don't blame you for jumping to conclusions and thinking I led you on. That's not what happened. I just reacted badly and could only think about my sister and my niece when I heard the news. I asked Jack not to tell you the whole story, just that I had a family emergency."

"He tried—but I didn't believe him," I said, remembering how badly I had reacted. "I thought it was a one night-stand to you."

He squeezed my hands. "It was never meant to be that. That's why when I came to my senses I told him to give you my contact information."

I shrugged. "Yeah, I ripped it up to shreds and then tossed his phone."

"Yeah, he made me pay for that. Literally. He made me buy him a new cellphone."

"Is it too late to tell him I'm sorry about that?"

He laughed. "I don't know, I don't think it's ever too late to tell someone you're sorry."

I knew he was talking about himself.

"I messed up, Nina. But I never stopped thinking about you. When you came to the office, I was speaking with a family lawyer trying to arrange custody of Rory. We were trying to track down my niece's father. It turns out that he didn't even know he had a daughter."

My heart dropped. "Oh really?"

"Yeah. Just further evidence of how selfish my sister is. The guy is actually a really decent person. He's from a nice hard-working family in Bakersfield. Good people. I met them, his parents and his brothers and sisters. They were so excited to meet Rory. They treat her like she's gold."

"So that's where your niece is now?"

"Yeah. She's with her dad. He has full custody. I see her on the weekends occasionally. She's having the time of her life. She has cousins and more grandparents now. She's so happy."

The very thing I was denying Sadie. The guilt I felt made me sick.

"Maybe your sister wasn't selfish. Maybe she had a reason for keeping her daughter a secret."

"I know my sister," he said letting go of my hand. "She probably did it out of spite."

"I think you're making light of the subject. Most women don't want to be a single mom…"

"I'm sure my sister didn't give it much thought, at all."

I found myself getting upset with him. "Cut her some slack, Griffin. And stop being so judgmental.... being a single mom is hard."

"Hey," he said. "I'm not arguing with you about that. But being a single mom was her choice. She could have told Vic, my niece's father."

"Maybe... maybe she was scared."

"Maybe, but I know my sister better than you do and don't forget she abandoned my niece to get high, so she's not exactly mother of the year."

"You're right, I don't know why I'm defending her."

"It's ok. I just don't know how someone could deliberately deny someone the right to be a father. I guess it's just upsetting because I loved my dad. I wouldn't have been the man I was without him."

I was glad for the change of subject. "Tell me about him."

Griffin took a sip of his wine and savored the taste as he thought of the past. "He was just your average Joe. He was actually my stepdad. I never had a relationship with my biological father. My parents divorced early and the visits from my biological dad became less and less frequent until one day he just stopped showing up altogether. I was angry a lot because of that. I was a very difficult child, if you let my mom tell it."

"I can believe that," I said lightly, enjoying the moment.

"Thanks," he said. "Anyway, so my mom remarried."

"Oh, so Jackson and your sister—"

"Nora."

"Yes, Nora. They're from your mom's second marriage?"

"Yep," he said. "So yeah, my stepdad was just this average guy, an adjunct professor at a small-time community college. I think my mom met him while on vacation. He had a normal job, nothing fancy. And so she married him and pretty much caused a scandal because he wasn't rich. He was just a nobody according to my mom's peers. But he was great—so great to me, to us. Just a kind, wonderful man with broad shoulders. I always felt he could take the world on those shoulders. He taught me what it was to be a man."

He grew silent and I didn't want to push, but I just had to know.

"What happened to him?"

"A car accident when I was about 13 or 14."

"I'm so sorry."

"A drunk driver killed him instantly. We were all devastated. It changed us, you know? Dad had been the glue that held us all together. And in that one instant, a stranger tore our family apart. Mom bore the worst of it. She retreated into herself and then when she got better, I don't think you could actually call it that, she became, what do they call it? A helicopter parent. She barely let us out of her sight. And my sister, she was a daddy's girl. After he died she was constantly butting heads with Mom. So stubborn, just like Mom. They couldn't see eye to eye and she left home at 16, running off with some friends. It took Mom a month to track her down and oh boy when she did, she rained down hell on my sister."

He shook his head.

"And Jackson?"

"He was the youngest, so he didn't know Dad as well

as the rest of us. He just tried to be the funny one, always making us laugh. Trying to get Mom to smile. He's the same way now, always trying to get the family together, always trying to make peace and get us to relax... come to think of it, he's a lot like Dad."

"I'm so sorry. I never knew my real father, but my stepdad is an amazing man. I can't imagine ever losing him."

"I wouldn't wish that pain on my worst enemy."

We sat in silence for a moment, each of us lost in thought.

"Did I ruin the evening by telling you all my family drama and secrets?" he asked as the waiter cleared our plates.

"No, not at all. I think we all have our share of secrets... things that we don't want others to know or just things that we don't want to talk about."

"What are your secrets, Nina?"

Now was the time. Just tell him, Nina. What happened to confident Nina? I hesitated. Tell him, Nina. But how to even begin?

"Griffin, there's something I need to tell you," I said, forcing the words out before I could change my mind.

"Uh oh, sounds serious," he joked.

The waiter took that moment to arrive with the check.

"Now, what were you saying?"

I lost my nerve. What if he saw me as selfish like his sister? I didn't want him to resent me. I needed time. I couldn't just spit it out. It just wasn't the right time.

"Nothing. I'm tired."

"Me too. I hate to sound like a stick in the mud, but I have an early meeting tomorrow."

"Aww... so you're done stalking me on set."

"My stalker days are over. After all, you agreed to have dinner with me so I think you're coming around."

He held out his hand to me and I took it. We walked out of the restaurant still holding hands. His nearness and the full moon reminded me of our moonlight tryst so long ago. It had been a balmy evening just like this one when I had crept into his room.

I looked at him and he looked at me, clearly we were thinking the same thing.

"Would it be too forward to invite you to my place?"

"Would it be too forward to accept?"

He smiled wickedly at me and opened the car door. I slid in, taking my time to rub against his body as I did.

"You're trouble, Nina."

"And you like it, Griffin."

I heard him chuckle as he closed the door. Nina Charles, what are you getting yourself into? I thought.

9

He pulled up to a high-rise in the middle of the city. It had a private parking garage and that was probably for the best, as I couldn't wait until we were out of the car.

I pulled myself into his lap and started kissing him as soon as he removed the key from the ignition. I couldn't get enough of him and apparently he couldn't get enough of me.

His hands went straight up my skirt and he started to massage me through my panties. I wriggled, shoving my hips forward, riding his hand that was doing delicious, dirty things.

I heard a tearing sound and realized he'd ripped my panties off and then abruptly he stopped.

"This garage has cameras," he said as in warning.

"Well, let them watch," was my reply before I kissed

him again, long and hard. He began fondling my breasts and I busied myself by unzipping his pants. There was a sense of urgency for both of us. I needed him in me, now. I wanted him so bad, and I'd been waiting years to have him if I were truthful with myself. This was the reason I hadn't even so much as had a date since Griffin... because my body craved him and only him.

I freed his length and stroked it boldly. He groaned.

"Are you ready for me Griffin?"

"I should be asking you that," he said, raising his hips up. I straddled him, spreading my legs as wide as they could go in the confined space of his SUV and slid myself down onto his dick.

He felt amazing. I moaned as he filled me, stretching me inch my inch. It had been a long time, and my body initially protested his entrance.

"You're so tight," he said, holding on to my upper waist, looking at me.

"It's been awhile," I said softly, cupping his face and kissing it as my inner muscles contracted and released around his dick. He groaned and I could feel him trying to control himself.

"God, you feel good."

"So, do you," I said as I began to ride him. I leaned back against the steering wheel and began to maneuver myself up and down, taking in a little at a time, until he was fully inside of me.

He grunted and grabbed my hips, slamming me down on his dick over and over while I played with my nipples, squeezing them and rubbing them against his face.

We were breathing heavily and I could feel myself about to come. He brought his hands up to squeeze my breasts and it was enough to send me quickly over the edge, and I came hard and fast.

So, fast that I was a little embarrassed. I collapsed against him and waited until my breathing slowed down before saying, "Sorry."

He laughed. "Isn't it the guy who normally apologizes for coming early?"

"It's 2017. New gender rules...."

"Oh, that explains a lot."

"You didn't come," I said, although I already knew the answer.

"There's still plenty of time for that."

When he pulled me off, my sex seemed to protest, but finally released him. I righted my dress and instantly felt exposed and vulnerable. What the hell did I just do?

"Umm... I suppose you'll want to head to bed now."

"Yep," he said. "With you. You said you would come over to my place, right? Well, we only made it to the parking garage. There's still plenty of time for other stuff."

I smiled at him and reached for my panties.

He stopped me. "You won't be needing those."

He straightened his clothes and I made sure I at least looked acceptable. He led me from the car to a private entrance that had an elevator only he could access. As soon as the elevator door closed, he stood in front of me and put his hand down my dress. He exposed one of my breasts, cupped it in his hand and licked and kissed the tip. I was so aroused, I could feel the wetness running down my thighs. But he wasn't done, he raised his mouth to mine and started kissing me and then his hand crept up my thigh... I spread my legs knowing what would come next when the elevator door rang, announcing we'd reached our destination.

I groaned in frustration when he took a step back and took my hand.

"We keep getting interrupted."

"It is a problem," he said succinctly and then he led me to his apartment door. As it clicked open, he picked me up.

I wrapped my arms around his neck and let him lead me to the bedroom. He placed me on the bed, but I couldn't see anything in front of me. It was hot, having sex in the dark.

I felt him spread my legs and then I felt his tongue slide between my wet folds and then he settled between my thighs, pushing them further apart as he knelt between them and sucked and licked between my legs.

I held his head in place and rocked my hips against his mouth, enjoying the feel of it, never wanting him to stop, but I was torn. I wanted him inside me again and I felt swollen in want.

He pulled away and reached up to turn on a light. Soft illumination filled the room as he pulled my dress off and tossed it to the side. My breasts spilled from my bra and he made no move to take it off. He stripped off his shirt and pants, and stroked his hand up and down his dick as he looked at me.

"You're still so beautiful," he said, staring down at me, as he sheathed himself in a condom.

I was grateful that the soft illumination most likely hid my stretch marks that were my battle scars from pregnancy. Other than that, my body hadn't changed much, except that my breasts were fuller and maybe my hips rounder.

"Open your legs for me," he said, and I slowly spread my legs wide.

He knelt down between my legs and pulled my hips under his and in one easy motion he pushed into me. He didn't waste any time as he went deeply into me, pulling out and then going deeper again.

I wrapped my legs around his back and bit into his shoulder as he leaned forward, covering my body with his own as he thrust into me over and over. I must have screamed too loudly, because he abruptly stopped moving and asked me if I were ok.

"Yes, don't stop…"

And then he kept pumping into me. My inner muscles squeezed his shaft, drawing it in deeper. He groaned.

"God, you're tight."

And I had every reason to be. I hadn't been with anyone since him.

He quickened his thrusts then, and the feel of his cock, thick and hard, sliding in and out of me pushed me over the edge. I screamed as he pumped into me, not sparing me as he drove deep and hard with each thrust until he too began to come.

We lay panting. I was breathless, but I still wanted more of him.

We lay with our faces next to each other and he brought a hand up to stroke my hip.

"You're curvier than I remember…" he remarked.

I pouted. "Are you calling me fat?"

"Not in a million years and even if you were… I'm not sure it would even matter to me."

I hadn't been expecting that. I'd just been teasing him, but apparently, he meant every word.

"You know I can't stay in L.A., right? Georgia is home."

"We don't have to talk about that now," he said, stroking my face. "In fact, we don't have to talk at all."

He surprised me by settling me on top of him and then turned me around until I was in reverse cowgirl position.

I could see his cock stirring again and I couldn't help but give it some much needed attention. I brought my head down and began to lick and suck at it, taking my time, enjoying the way I turned him on. He responded by stroking and massaging my butt, and then he rotated his hips so he was now on his side and I flipped to my side to keep him in my mouth. My head was directly in front of his crotch and my crotch was near his face. He began fingering me and licking my clit as I brought his dick again into my mouth.

I could barely concentrate on pleasuring him as he pleasured me, opening me up wider with his hand as he lazily licked circles around my clit.

My body began to shake and the next thing I knew, Griffin was abandoning his post between my legs and instead was flipping me over.

I knew what he wanted so I waited patiently as he put on another condom and then I buried my head in a pillow as he pushed into me from behind.

He slapped my ass, making me giggle and then I quickly became serious blindly reaching for a rail as he pounded into me. He was merciless and I loved it. It was hard, almost animalistic the way he fucked me and I wanted more... needed more.

"Griffin, please Griffin..."

He paused as I moaned his name, and pulled out of me ever so slowly. I gripped the sheets of the bed in my fists.

"Griffin. Please... more... put it back in..."

"You sure? You look a little tired," he teased, inserting the tip of his dick into my wet, pulsating vagina.

I shivered at the feel of it and licked my dry lips. "Fuck me, Griffin... please..."

I didn't care that I was begging. I wanted him so fucking bad.

"I love it when you beg," he said, pushing in just a little bit further. I was so wet, I knew all I had to do was rock back just a little and his whole long, thick length would be inside me. But I liked this teasing, this prolonging the inevitable. It made fucking Griffin all that much more desirable. And that's all this was, right? Just sex? Just really good sex.

I didn't get to contemplate it too long, as he pushed into me and began to move slowly in and out, taking his time, letting himself become acquainted with every inch of my wet, clenching opening. His dick was hot, as it filled me and I tilted my hips up greedily for more.

"You like that?"

"Yes, Griffin," I moaned.

"God, you're tight... so tight... and wet."

He moaned this time as he plunged himself into me again. And then we were both beyond words as he grabbed my hips and began to thrust into me recklessly. I screamed as pleasure and pain became one... as he pushed so deeply I thought he would tear right through me, but yet, it wasn't enough. God, I wanted more. So much more.

Griffin gave me what I wanted by rubbing my clit with one hand as he continued to pound into me.

The room was filled with the sound of our breathing and the sound of his body slapping against mine as he rode me hard from behind. I knew I was coming again, my body beginning to shake. I closed my eyes as my orgasm radiated from where Griffin was teasing my clit with his finger to my vagina where his cock was stretching and filling me, sending waves of pleasure that seized my entire body, making my head pound and my skin tingle.

As I came, I screamed, squeezing his penis with my walls. He slid in and out of my wetness, still hard, still pumping and I came again, luxuriating in the feel of him sliding into my wetness over and over again, as my muscles quivered around him.

And finally, he came, driving deeply into me one more time, sending his hot, piercing dick into me and holding it there while he groaned my name.

He pulled out of me and I collapsed forward, sighing heavily into a pillow. My insides were still quivering from the aftermath of our lovemaking.

He chuckled and I could only imagine the sight I made, naked and spent, lying on his pillows with my bra haphazardly aligned.

As if finally noticing, he unhooked it and placed a chaste kiss on my back, which served to make me shiver. He kissed my back again and I moaned. He tossed my bra elsewhere and turned me over. He climbed on top of me, but held himself up on one elbow.

He touched my face, tracing a finger down my cheek. "You okay?"

"Better than okay," I whispered. I stared into his eyes and he stared into mine.

"I guess now we're reacquainted."

"I think so."

He kissed me again, sweetly. "I could kiss you all day."

"And I would let you."

"Yeah, I can't imagine you objecting to being kissed all day."

I made a face at him and he playfully pinched my butt. "Ouch!"

He laughed. "You like it..."

He made his way to the bathroom and I sat up a little to watch him walk away. No wonder his thrusts felt so powerful, I thought to myself as I looked at his naked butt. He had a behind that anyone, man or woman, would envy. It was so perfect.

His perfect butt disappeared into the bathroom and I realized then that I was completely naked and had nothing to put on besides my old dress. I covered myself with the blanket and settled into his soft luxurious pillows.

I felt him crawl into bed with me and I remarked, "It must be so nice being rich. You one-percenters have the best pillows."

"Nice pillows are a requirement or you get kicked out the billionaire club."

"Now you wouldn't want that," I joked lazily, ready to doze off.

My eyes were closing as he wrapped his arms around me and pulled me towards his chest.

"It's Grant, by the way."

"Hmm?"

"My name...G.L. Wallace? It's Grant Leonard Wallace. That's my full name."

"That's a nice respectable name, but I like Griffin better."

He chuckled and I cuddled against his chest, feeling safe and warm. A feeling that, as I dozed off, I realized I could get used to.

## 10

The next morning, I stretched out my legs and took a deep breath. I woke up slowly, forgetting where I was, trying to nestle myself deeper into the covers. The sun was peeking through the blinds and I tried to bury my head under a pillow when I heard a beep.

It was a familiar beep, but in my sleepy state it took a while for me to recognize it.

"My phone," I said to mostly myself as I picked it up. I had a text message. It was from my mom.

It simply said, "Just texting to see if you're ok. You forgot to call last night." And attached was a picture of Mom, Sadie and Dad together in front of the breakfast table. It was a terrible attempt at a selfie and it made me laugh.

I felt guilty at first that I'd gotten so wrapped up last

night that I'd forgotten to call, but then I squelched that guilt. It wasn't like I'd been caught being irresponsible with a complete stranger. I'd just got swept away by my child's father.

I texted her back that I was sorry and that I would call soon, then scoured the floor for my bra and dress. I found them and slipped them on.

Where the heck was Griffin?

I made my way out of the bedroom and ran into a tall figure.

"Hey, you! Long time no see!"

Oh, God. Not this again. It was Jackson.

I opened my mouth to greet him when I felt two hands grab me by the waist and pull me back against a hard chest I instantly recognized as Griffin's. He hugged me from behind, holding me possessively as he spoke to Jackson.

"Didn't I tell you to stay in the kitchen?" Griffin said to Jackson.

"I had to pee," Jackson whined.

"There's a lady in the room, for God's sake Jackson, watch your language."

Jackson looked contrite. "Sorry. But I did have to pee. You're looking good... errr... sorry, what was your name again?" I opened my mouth to tell him when he interrupted again. "Nina! That's it!"

His phone beeped and he reached for it, giving me a

wide grin. "I'm keeping this one far away from you. Phone killer." He walked away as he began to talk on the phone. "Hey, hun! Yeah, yeah... I'm over at my brother's. Remember that girl I told you about who went berserk and tossed my phone... she's here! No, seriously, she is. She and Griffin are back together. You know he always liked the crazy ones..." he said, disappearing into a room.

Griffin looked at me and I looked at him and we both snickered.

"Your brother just called me crazy. I didn't go berserk. He's exaggerating."

"Well, I don't know about that."

I punched Griffin playfully in the shoulder. He caught my hand and brought it up to his lips to kiss the back of it.

"Did you sleep well?" He asked meeting my eyes and giving me a sexy look.

I gave him one of my own and said, "The little sleep I had was enjoyable..."

"Are you complaining?" he teased, leading me to a barstool at the giant quartz island in his kitchen.

"No."

"I would hope not, you're the insatiable one that kept waking me up. I should be the exhausted one."

I couldn't help but blush in the daylight. He was right. I can't remember how many other times I had woken up to initiate sex with him all over again. It had been a delicious evening... one I definitely would never forget. One I'd love to repeat, but first, I had to tell him the truth.

"Griffin, remember the other night when I said we needed to talk?"

"God, I hope this isn't about Jerry because if you tell me you're in love with him, I swear I'm going to throw him from a building."

"Why are you so obsessed with Jerry?"

"Isn't it simple? He's into you. I can't have another man sniffing at my woman."

I raised my eyebrows. So, I was his woman now? Interesting.

"Jerry is just a friend. And you and I only became 'reacquainted' last night."

"And what a good night that was," he said jokingly, giving me a lewd wink.

I couldn't' help but laugh. "You're ridiculous."

"Don't I know it."

The doorbell rang and Griffin looked annoyed. "I'm not expecting anyone. Be right back. Watch these eggs for me, I hate overcooked eggs." He muttered almost to himself as he walked to the door.

He wasn't wearing a shirt, just flannel pajama bottoms that hugged his backside in the most appealing way. I liked the way his back muscles moved with his every step. Apparently, while I got curvier, Griffin got sexier... sometimes it's not fair being a woman. I popped a small piece of an egg in my mouth and added another. I was starving.

He went to open the door when the door opened up on its own and Mrs. Wallace came striding in.

"It's almost noon... why don't you have any clothes on? I didn't raise you to be a heathen—" She stopped abruptly as she caught sight of me.

"You! What are you doing here?"

I opened my mouth to speak and the words came out as gibberish because my mouth was full of eggs.

She turned to Griffin and said, "What is she doing here?"

"She has every right to be here, Mom. Calm down," Griffin said more fiercely than I would have expected.

"I will not calm down!" she said, marching past him and coming within inches of me. "You just don't give up, do you? Do I have to pay you off again? Why won't you just leave him alone?"

I looked at Griffin who looked at me curiously.

"Pay you off?" He said to me and then looked at his mom, "What are you talking about?"

"I paid her $250,000 to leave you alone. And she took the money and apparently is back for more."

"What?"

"That's not true," I said, finally able to defend myself now that I was done chewing.

"Oh, really? Then explain where the $250,000 went."

I gulped hard. "I used it."

"You see!" his mom said victoriously.

Griffin looked at me as if he'd never seen me before. I felt humiliated and vulnerable... the same way I felt all those years ago when Mrs. Wallace had lied to me about Griffin having a family. And then it occurred to me that because of her lies, my daughter hadn't known her father. It was because of her lies that my daughter didn't know her uncle or know that she had a cousin and another one on the way. I was done with Mrs. Wallace scheming.

"It's true, your mom paid me $250,000 to make me go away."

"And you took it," Griffin said emotionlessly. I felt my eyes tearing up, but I was determined to not let her win this time.

"What your mother didn't mention is why... ask her why I left. She led me to believe a lie."

She glared at me and turned to Griffin. "I told you already, Griffin. This is why I had security escort her out. I just wanted to protect you from her, I knew she was bad news. Not our kind, at all."

"And what exactly is our kind, Mom?" Griffin growled.

"Griffin, I—"

"Stop. Dad wasn't our kind, and yet you married him."

Her lips grew tight. "This isn't about your father."

"In a way, I think it is. From what I understand, you went out of your way to make sure Nina never got to me."

"I did what was best. She's a predator. A gold digger."

"Stop, Mom. Just stop—"

"You heard her! She took my money! She doesn't have a conscience! I paid her off for cheap!" she spit out, her voice growing shrill. She was finally losing her composure and we stared at her. As if realizing it, she straightened her shoulders and slipped a hand through her perfectly coiffed hair. "Ask her," she finally said.

Griffin turned to me. There was no accusation in his eyes. In fact, he just looked tired. His eyes were guarded, but he looked exhausted as if he had had all he could take emotionally for one day. Apparently, Mrs. Wallace was always a handful.

"She implied that you had a family. So yes, I took the money. I... I needed it."

"See there! I told you," she said.

"You lied to her and told her that I had a family?" Griffin said.

"Not exactly. I might have implied it but she drew her own conclusions."

"You're lying! You did more than imply."

She shook her head. "Who are you going to believe? Some floozy that whored herself on an island or me?"

"Woah, woah, woah," said Jackson cutting in. "I told you, Mom, they were entertainment specialists. Not whores."

If she hadn't been implying that I was a whore, Jackson's interjection would have been funny.

"If it walks like a duck, talks like a duck and acts like a duck, Jackson, then it's a duck," Mrs. Wallace said coldly.

"Or a goose... they look a lot alike," Jackson quipped.

"Shut up, Jackson," Mrs. Wallace snarled. Jackson promptly excused himself.

"Mom, you have to stop," Griffin said ignoring Jackson.

"Stop? Stop what?"

"Interfering with our lives."

"Interfering? Me helping you avoid a scandal is what you consider interference? Me trying to get the rubbish out of your life is a disaster?"

"I'm not garbage," I growled, finding my voice.

"You're right. You're way worse than that. At least garbage knows its place."

I was done talking. I was ready to strangle that old lady. I jumped down from my barstool and was making my way over to her when Griffin stepped in between us.

I knew then that it was time to tell Griffin everything.

"After she called security on me, I gave Cliff my number and contact information. She must have got it from him because she arranged to meet up with me at an ice cream shop on the beach. I thought I was meeting up with you, but she turned up instead with the $250, 000."

"So I lied. I was just trying to protect you from the ugliness of life. Is that so bad? Why do I feel like I'm on trial here? I did nothing wrong," she screeched.

"I saw you playing on the beach with a little girl and I saw you hug a woman. I thought you had used me, especially after you left so abruptly."

Griffin looked confused and then turned to his mom and said, "How could you?"

"What?"

"You took her to the ice cream shop at the beach? The one we used to go to with Dad every weekend? You took her there to do your dirty work?"

"I did what I had to do." Mrs. Wallace was stoic, her expression gave away nothing of what she was feeling.

"I know the beach and ice cream shop you're talking about. Our dad used to take us there every weekend, I thought it would be nice to take my niece and my friend... the woman you saw me hugging. I'll never forget that day, because my niece met her father that day. It was a special day for her so I wanted it to take place somewhere that had been special to me... special to all of us."

Griffin's mom's lips grew so tight they were barely perceptible. She sat down on the couch and pleaded with Griffin yet again. "I just did what I thought was best."

"I know and that's why it's so sad. You thought keeping me away from someone I cared about was good for me. Think about that, Mom."

She shook her head. "Nora had already caused enough pain with her bad decision-making. I just didn't want to go down that road again."

"Yes, because keeping up appearances is so much more important than your kids' happiness."

She narrowed her eyes at him. "That's not true and you know it. Your happiness, Jackson's, even Nora's means more to me than my own."

"Oh stop, you're no saint, Mom."

"Neither is she!" she yelled, pointing at me. "You think you're the only man she's seeing?"

I furrowed my brows. "What the hell are you talking about? More lies?" I looked at Griffin who placed his hands on his hips and looked down at the floor shaking his head as if he couldn't believe the words coming out of her mouth.

"Mom, you're off your rocker."

She became livid and leaped up from her chair. "I saw her a few days ago cuddled up with some guy at the gym! Ask her if you don't believe me." She turned to me and said, "And don't you try to deny it."

"There's nothing to deny," I said with a carefree shrug, "You did see me with a guy... my cousin Kenny. He's an instructor there."

"A likely story—"

"Not another word. You've said enough," Griffin interrupted in a cold voice. She finally had his undivided attention.

She swallowed thickly. "You're going to take her word over mine."

He said softly, "Mom... I haven't been able to take you at your word since Dad died."

She pulled her face back as if he had just slapped her. "Ok, I see. I'll just leave now." She stood up slowly and walked to the door as if she wanted him to stop her, as if she was giving him the chance to tell her not to go. She was sorely mistaken.

"Ok, well, call me when your world falls apart. Because with her, that's the only future you have. A future that's worth nothing."

With that parting shot, she got into the elevator and was gone.

"Is she gone?" Jackson said, sticking his head out.

Griffin closed the door silently, not answering.

Jackson happily sat down on the couch and said, "Hey, I don't blame you. If she offered me $250,000 I would have taken it."

I flinched. "I didn't want to take it, I tried to give it back to her—"

"Jackson," Griffin interrupted. "Go home. I need to talk to Nina alone."

I swallowed hard. I should have known I wasn't getting off that easily.

"Oh," he said, sounding disappointed, "I guess I should head home then."

"Yeah, you should," Griffin said softly. I could hear the anger bubbling under the surface and apparently so could Jackson.

Jackson abruptly hugged me and whispered, "You're on your own, babe. Sorry."

I sighed, knowing he was right. Griffin grabbed him by the shoulder and practically shoved him out the door.

"Hey! This jacket is expensive!" was the last I heard from Jackson as Griffin slammed the door.

I sat down heavily on the couch and he sat across from me.

"Did you plan to tell me?"

"About which part?" I said deliberately coy.

"The money..."

"Oh, that part."

"Is that why you came back to see me that day in the office? You wanted money?"

"What? No! That's not why!"

"Because Jackson said you wanted nothing to do with me when I left the island. And then suddenly you showed up months later, just out of the blue..."

"Listen, I know how it looks, but that's not what happened."

"Isn't it?"

"I mean, yeah, I was angry with you after you left me on the island. I thought there was something more between us and when I woke up and you weren't there, I was really hurt—"

"I already told you what happened."

"Yes, years later."

"But that still doesn't explain why you showed up months later, that does sound suspicious."

I was speechless. He thought that lowly of me? Really? I took a deep breath and tried to stay cool and collected. Don't get emotional, Nina.

"I'm sorry if that seems suspicious, but I was not after your money."

"But yet when Mom offered it, you took it."

"I needed it."

"You needed it?"

"Yes," I said refusing to meet his eyes. "I didn't ask for it. I tried to give it back, but I eventually needed it."

"Where's the money now, Nina?" he asked coldly. "Spent it all? Got yourself some pretty things? Maybe a fancy car?"

I looked up at him sharply. "You know me better than that."

"Actually, no. No, I don't. I know my mother is a misguided snob, but I don't know your angle."

"I don't have one."

He nodded and then stood up. He began to pace. "I think it's time that we put all our cards on the table, so to speak."

I gulped, knowing there was one card I was holding that would trump all other cards.

"Do you want to go first?"

I shook my head.

"Ok, then I'll go." He abruptly stopped pacing and leaned against a pillar. "I had Richard offer you the insurance commercial job. It wasn't a coincidence. I wanted to see you again so I told him to hire you. He didn't just happen to "share" with me that you were in town. I had him bring you here."

His confession didn't surprise me. I'd already put that together.

"So, is that why your mom was at the casting for the entertainment specialist job? She didn't think Richard would do a good job?" I asked, stalling.

"Pretty much. She wanted to make sure Jackson and

I weren't around any girls that would cause a scandal."

That had been my initial thought. It made perfect sense and it explained so much. I bet Richard had picked me against his aunt's wishes and had deliberately paired me up with Griffin to shake things up. Well, he certainly accomplished that.

But that's not what this conversation was about.

"I guess now it's my turn."

"I guess," is all he said. I couldn't read his expression.

"After the island, our encounter on the island, I was depressed and so I left to lick my wounds, so to speak. I went back home and I..." I stopped, not knowing what to say or how to say it.

"You realized who I was and that you could get very good money from my family?"

"No! How could you think that?" I said.

He shrugged. "It's the most logical conclusion. You were a broke actress. I'm set to inherit hundreds of millions over what I already have now. What conclusion would you come up with?"

He was right. All conclusions led to me being one gold-digging you-know-what. But I thought Griffin knew better than that. Apparently not.

I tried to speak calmly and keep my voice from shaking, but I was visibly upset. "I might have been a struggling actress, but I have some dignity."

"Yes, enough to take $250,000."

"If I had only had to worry about me, I would not have taken it," I said angrily.

"What is that supposed to mean?" he said staring at me.

I closed my eyes, took a deep breath, and opened them. "I was pregnant. With your baby. That's why I took the money. I didn't ask for it but when your mom wouldn't take it back and I saw you with that woman and that child, I don't know... I thought that I was doing the right thing. I knew I would need money and like you said, I was just a broke actress."

I expected him to yell at me or say something, anything. His silence was killing me. He was staring off into the distance as if I didn't even exist anymore.

"Griffin?"

"Get out."

"What?" I hadn't expected that. He looked at me and his eyes were cold, flat and emotionless.

"Get out," he repeated simply.

"I tried to tell you earlier—I swear I did." I didn't understand why he was angry and then I thought back to the conversation we had about his sister Nora.

"Go," he said softly. He walked to the door and held it open. "Get out."

I wanted to fight him. I wanted to yell at him. I wanted to do something, but I did what I thought was best, which was nothing. I walked past him, determined not to show how much pain I was in and I walked out the door. He slammed it behind me, so hard that the noise it caused scared me to the point that I let out a startled cry.

As the elevator came for me, I tried to tell myself to not cry. I tried to tell myself that everything would be fine. I'd done what I was supposed to do. And now it was time to go home.

I reached for my phone and realized I'd left it in Griffin's place. I would have just walked away, but I didn't have a way to get home. I'd left my wallet and everything in Griffin's place.

I marched to his door and banged on it, not caring if my banging disturbed the neighbors.

"I left my phone and my wallet," I said when he answered the door looking angry.

Without a word, I barged around him and found my phone ringing in his bedroom. I grabbed it and my purse.

At least now I can answer my phone without worrying about him finding out my secret, I thought to myself as I answered, walking past Griffin. The secret was officially out in the open, but for some reason, I didn't feel any better than before. I got into the elevator and I tried not to think of the pain I felt, that made it hard to even breathe.

I wiped away tears and tried to keep my voice cheerful as I spoke into the phone, "Hi, Mom. How's—"

"You have to come home—"

My heart dropped to the pit of my stomach. "Why? What's wrong?"

Her cellular reception was going in and out. "Mom... Mom?"

"Hon... hospital... come home," were the last words I heard before the line went dead.

$\mathcal{I}$ awoke from a hard sleep when I heard someone pull the curtain back beside the hospital bed. I'd spent the night curled up in the chair next to the gigantic hospital bed and my body felt cramped, but I ignored the soreness of my body as I looked towards the person now peering at me. I'd spent most of the night worrying, pacing, praying, hoping for a miracle.

And this morning I'd gotten exactly the miracle I hoped for as I rubbed my eyes and saw him sitting up in bed.

"Hi, Dad. How are you feeling?"

"Felt better yesterday. I barely slept. You were snoring so loud I thought about having the nurses remove you."

"I guess that means you're feeling better."

"I would if I could get this dang curtain down. Makes me feel dead having this curtain around me."

"Wow, Dad. You just had a stroke, leave the curtain alone."

"A stroke? I feel fine."

"You might feel fine but the doctors want you to take it easy."

"They're trying to kill me."

"I'm pretty sure they're not."

"You're too trusting."

"You're too ornery."

"I hate doctors."

"Mom's a doctor."

"She's the exception to the rule. Where is she by the way?"

I didn't answer. I stood up and wrapped my arms around him. He sat stiffly before finally hugging me back.

I felt tears falling down my face and plopping on the top of his bald shiny head. "Are you crying or did the ceiling just spring a leak?"

"Both," I teased. Reluctantly, I let him go.

"Stop the crying," he said, looking around for a handkerchief. He always kept a handkerchief in his pocket. That was a difficult feat when wearing a hospital gown. I grossed him out by using the sleeve of my shirt.

"I'm going to pretend that I didn't see that," he said, lying back down.

"But seriously, how are you feeling?"

"Just tired. Did they say when I can leave?"

"A few days, I think. They want to run some more tests."

"That's because I have insurance. The good kind. If I didn't they would have just made sure I was alive and sent me on my way."

Dad was such a cynic.

"I need to get home to Sadie, but I'll be back. Mom should be on her way."

"Who's watching Sadie?" he asked, trying to sit up again.

I stopped him. "Relax, Dad. Kenny's here."

He smiled. "Kenny? He's going to have her sashaying up and down the hallway like she's a runway model. And then who will I have around to play checkers with? He's going to turn her into a diva."

"I promise Kenny won't do any permanent damage," I teased.

"He'd better not. That Kenny," Dad said, chuckling.

"Get some rest. I'll see you soon."

He grunted and then soon enough he was snoring. I stood staring down at him and slowly took his hand in mine. I squeezed it and he surprised me by squeezing back.

"Love you, Daddy," I said, kissing his forehead before making my way out.

I almost ran into my mom who looked frazzled.

"Hi, honey. How's he looking?"

"About the same."

"Ok. Thanks for staying with him. I had a long night. Full moon and all that." My mom swore that the full moon brought out all the weirdos and as an emergency room physician, she'd seen her share of weird things.

"You know I don't mind staying longer."

"No," she said giving me a light push towards the elevator. "Go home to your daughter. I'll stay with your father."

I knew there was no point in arguing with her. When her mind was made up, there was no point in trying to change it.

I got on the elevator and sighed as I pushed the down button. I was so tired. As soon as I had gotten off the elevator at Griffin's place, I'd called my mom back, feeling frantic.

She'd told me with tears in her voice that she'd found Dad unconscious and was waiting for the attending physician to give her an update. I hadn't hesitated. I'd gone directly from Griffin's house to the airport and called Kenny on the way.

He dropped whatever he was doing and had joined me as we waited for the flight back to Georgia. We'd held hands like scared little kids as we waited for our flight. We barely spoke, both deep in thought, and worried about my dad. We were a close-knit family. Worrying about each other is what we did best.

When we had landed, we'd stopped at my mom's house to relieve the sitter. Kenny had volunteered to stay with a sleeping Sadie until I came back.

Mom couldn't find anyone to cover for her at work so she'd been stuck working while Dad was in the hospital. Luckily, it was the same hospital she worked for.

And now I was on my way back to Mom's house to get Sadie and relieve Kenny.

Home was only ten minutes from the hospital and when I pulled up, I saw Kenny chasing behind Sadie. They were jumping over my dad's pond full of his precious koi, chasing each other with water guns.

"Mom!" Sadie yelled when she saw me. She dropped the gun and ran full speed into me, knocking the wind out of me in the process.

"Wow! I guess you missed me!"

"I missed you so, so, so, so, so much," she said, hugging me tightly.

"I missed you so, so, so, so, so much, too," Kenny said, smiling brightly as he blasted me with a spray of cold water.

"Kenny!"

"Ha! Just like old times!" he yelled, blasting me again.

"Watch this, Sadie," I said, bending down to retrieve her weapon as I mercilessly let Kenny have it. He hit the ground and tried to crawl away.

I stood over him and soaked him with the remaining water in the gun.

"I give up! I give up!" he yowled, and Sadie watched it all while laughing deep belly laughs.

"Mom, you're silly."

"She's the worst!" Kenny yelled from his position on the ground.

"Hey, you want more?"

"Didn't I tell you?" Kenny said raising himself up on his elbows, addressing Sadie.

"Tell her what?" I said, looking at him suspiciously.

"Your mom loves to beat me up."

"Oh my gosh, *we* beat each other up. Don't listen to him, Sadie."

I helped Kenny up even though I wanted to push him back down, and together the three of us covered in dirt and water made our way inside Mom's house.

"God, this place brings back so many memories. Remember how short we were and when we wanted to drink water from the faucet we had to put our feet on the vanity and lean over?"

I nodded. "We weren't that much older than Sadie is now."

"Those were the best of times."

We placed Sadie in front of the television and made our way to the kitchen to talk.

"So, how is he?" Kenny asked, putting his hands in his pockets and looking at me anxiously.

"Stable... he's stable. They want to run some tests, but the worst is over."

"Do they know how it happened?"

I shrugged. "I don't know, no one really talked to me." I felt helpless and useless. I felt like a little girl, even though I was raising one of my own.

Kenny held out his arms and I stepped into them. He hugged me tight and rested his chin on top of my head.

"We'll get through this together. He'll be fine. You'll see. He has all of us. He'll be fine."

I squeezed my eyes closed, hoping to God that Kenny was right.

And then I felt arms circling my waist and realized that Sadie had joined us in a group hug. I couldn't help but laugh.

"You feel left out?"

She shrugged. "Maybe a little."

I picked her up and hugged her tight. "You can head to the H-O-S-P-I-T-A-L. We'll be ok," I said to Kenny looking over my shoulder at him.

"You sure?"

"Positive."

He ruffed up my hair and then Sadie's and left.

"So... what should we do now?" I said to Sadie, so happy to be home even though the situation was less than ideal.

"Make brownies?"

"Yum yum, brownies. Sounds like a plan."

I placed her down and thought again how wonderful it was to be home.

Four hours later, Sadie was taking a nap next to me on the couch. I was reading a book, or at least trying to. My focus was off and I found myself staring at the wall, worrying about Dad. I texted Kenny, but he hadn't gotten back to me yet. I didn't want to call Mom because I was sure she was busy with Dad.

I laid Sadie down on the couch and started cleaning. I needed to keep busy or else I would go insane. I heard a car pull up in my driveway and looked out the window, expecting to see Kenny, but it was Mom's car.

She climbed out slowly, looking tired. I opened the door and waited on the porch for her. She climbed the steps looking weary and beat down.

She didn't notice me standing there with the door open until she was almost on top of me. "Oh, wow... I didn't even see you standing there."

"You're tired," I said, stepping out of the way as she entered the house.

She collapsed on a chair in the sitting room and

sighed. "Nina," she said tiredly, "don't get married. I swear your dad made me sprout seven new gray hairs today. And all on my chin. Don't tell anyone that. My hairy secret goes to the grave, got it?"

"Got it," I said with a small smile, happy that she could still joke at a time like this.

"How are you doing, Mom? How are you holding up?" I sat down in the little antique chair across from her.

"I'm doing ok. Your dad is driving me crazy. He's the worst patient."

"Yeah, I can imagine that. You know how cranky he gets when he's sick."

"Oh yeah, he hates being fawned over as he calls it. He slaps at the nurses' hands, tells off the doctors. He's just a handful."

"That's Daddy for you."

She smiled. "He's going to be fine. It's my reputation at the hospital that I'll have to worry about. They might all hate me just by association."

"Guilty by association."

"Yeah, your dad is getting quite the reputation and dragging me down with him," she laughed.

"So, he's going to be alright?"

"Yep. He might need a few physical therapy sessions, but otherwise he'll be fine. I'll have to change his diet."

"Oh nooo!"

"That's what he said. No more steaks and potatoes. Veggies and fish from now on."

"He's going to have to cancel all his outdoor parties."

My dad planned outdoor parties every summer and invited nearly everyone in the neighborhood and everyone who visited the neighborhood. One year the postman had shown up, the FedEx driver and the man who maintained some of the local yards.

"I'm glad he's going to be alright. I'm also glad I'm home."

"Speaking of which, I'm sorry, I just panicked. I should have waited to call you. I'm a doctor yet I panicked!" she said with disbelief in her voice.

"Well, for the first time it was you who was the family of the patient. Don't be so hard on yourself."

"Did you lose your job because of me?"

I shook my head. "We were done filming." She paused and I could easily guess what was coming next. "So did you talk to him?"

I didn't play coy. I knew who she was talking about.

"Yep."

"And?"

"It didn't go well. His mother showed up and pretty much made sure that he thought the worst of me... not to mention his sister had a daughter and never told the father. And he, of course, resents his sister for that."

"Yikes."

"Yeah, so he's not too thrilled about me now."

Mom sighed. "So, what happens now?"

"I put all this behind me and try to be the best mom I can be despite the circumstances."

She nodded, her eyes showing me without words how proud of me she was. "You're resilient, Nina, whether you give yourself credit or not. When the going gets tough, you don't just buckle under pressure. Sadie's lucky that you're her mom."

I teared up a little and swiped at my eyes. "You're going to make me cry!"

She waved her hands in the air and said, "Sorry... this family has done enough crying these past few days. Come on, let's go make some brownies."

"You sound like your granddaughter."

"Well, that little girl has a good head on her shoulders, courtesy of her grandma."

We laughed and headed into the kitchen, grateful beyond words that Dad would be fine.

THE NEXT DAY I woke up in my own bed and stretched. It wasn't a king size bed like Griffin's, but it was cheap and comfortable. At the time when I bought it, those had been my only requirements.

I rolled over and found Sadie right next to me. She

was wide awake playing with her wooden alphabets. She was lining them up in order and practicing the sounds that each letter made. In between each sound, she sang a little song.

She was just as smart as she was adorable. I sat up and pointed to one of the letters, letting out a big yawn.

"What letter is that?" I said after I was done yawning.

"B!" she said excitedly.

"And what sound does it make?"

"Buh—buh-buh," she said.

"Good job, and what words start with B?"

She stared at the letter and then said, "Bus... baby... balloon."

I held my hand out. "High-five! Good job!"

She gave me a high-five and continued organizing her letters.

I heard a noise from elsewhere in the house and then I instantly relaxed. I had forgotten for a moment that Kenny was still staying with us.

"Let's go get breakfast."

"I ate eggs. And toast. Already," she said not looking up.

Of course, Kenny had cooked. He just loved making me look bad, I thought sourly.

It was then that I could smell hints of spices coming from the kitchen. I left Sadie playing and ventured to the kitchen.

Bacon. Eggs. Pork chops smothered in gravy. Grits and biscuits. There were even sausages.

"Kenny, what's up with this feast?"

"Happiness," came a voice from behind me and I let out a surprised shriek. I turned around and saw a familiar face. I hugged him instantly.

"Cyril! It's so good to see you! What are you doing here?"

"When Kenny didn't answer his phone I knew something must be wrong. You know how he's always attached to it. Anyway, so when I finally reached him I knew he couldn't handle this alone, so I flew in."

"That's so sweet," I said.

"I know. I'm a sweet guy," Cyril said, and I couldn't suppress my smile.

"Where's Kenny now?"

"He said he had to go to town for something. He'll be back."

I was helping myself to a second helping of eggs and Sadie was chowing down on a muffin when Kenny's car pulled up.

He got out and the expression on his face looked guilty. Confused, I stood up and walked towards the window. And then another car pulled up right behind him. I didn't recognize it.

"Who's that?" Cyril asked.

I shrugged. "I'm not expecting any visitors."

The car stopped right next to Kenny's and Kenny patiently waited for whoever it was to get out.

My fists balled up and my heart rate picked up when I saw who had dared come to my house.

"Who's the good looking dude?" Cyril inquired standing next to me peering out the window.

"Griffin..."

"Sadie's fath—"

I sent him a look, not wanting Sadie to overhear.

"Sadie, why don't you go play dolls with Cyril? You can show him your doll house."

"Ok," she said. "Come on. It's awesome."

"I had a doll house when I was your age," I could hear him say as they disappeared down the hall.

I wiped my face and opened the front door. Kenny looked at me guiltily as I came out onto the porch.

"It's not my fault," were the first words out of his mouth.

"I don't want to hear it. Go inside, Kenny."

He looked at me and then at Griffin, and then shrugged his shoulders and did as he was told.

"What are you doing here, Griffin?"

"I wanted to see you."

"Really? I find that hard to believe."

"I'm sorry for how I handled things. I messed up. I want to talk."

"It's too late for that," I said, turning around, ready to go back into the house.

It was then that I saw Sadie standing there, staring at us through the window.

He noticed her too and stared, anchored to that spot. I pushed at him. "Get in your car now. Let's go."

He finally woke up out of his brief moment of shock and got in the car. I climbed in next to him and said curtly, "Drive."

"Where?"

"Just drive!" I shouted. I was a ball of nerves and I knew I was being irrational. Griffin didn't know where to go in town. He wasn't from here.

"Yes, ma'am," he said softly.

"She's the spitting image of my little sister," he said after a while. "We don't even have the same father, but she looks just like Nora."

I didn't comment. I was too busy texting Kenny to keep an eye on Sadie.

He texted back, "I already have that covered. Good luck!"

I sat back and rested my head against the headrest. And then I abruptly sat up. "What the hell was that all about, Griffin? What the hell were you thinking showing up like that?" I was close to shouting, but managed to keep my voice down. It was a struggle to say the least.

"Yeah, I messed up."

"How did you know where I was? Or where I lived?"

"That part was easy. Richard gave me your address."

"Richard is terrible with confidentiality."

"Yeah, you can't trust him."

"No kidding."

"Anyway, he gave me your address, but I was still having trouble finding you so I stopped in town and ran into Kenny at the grocery store when I stopped to ask for directions."

"And of course he led you to me."

"Well, he tried to pretend that he didn't see me. He hid behind his jacket and tried to sneak out, which made him even more noticeable... so don't be too mad at him."

The image he conjured of Kenny sneaking around trying to look inconspicuous would have made me laugh on a normal day. Today wasn't a normal day.

"I'm going to be honest with you, I'm too emotionally spent to talk to you right now. My dad is in the hospital, my mom needs me. I don't have the luxury of playing house with you right now."

He winced. "What happened to your dad?"

"He had a stroke. I don't want to talk about it."

"Is he okay?"

"I said I don't want to talk about it." It came out more forcefully than I'd intended.

"Ok..."

We drove in silence and finally I gave in. "He's going to be fine. He'll just need physical therapy and a diet change."

"Yikes."

"That's what I said. The man loves pork chops smothered in gravy."

"Well, for what it's worth, I'm glad he's going to be alright. I know how much you love him." He glanced at me and said, "Should I just keep driving in circles?"

"I don't know." Suddenly I realized that I honestly didn't know. I didn't know what was next for my dad or my mom. I didn't know what was next for Kenny and Cyril. And I didn't know what was next for me and Sadie. So maybe I had to deal with the here and now... which meant dealing with Griffin.

"I know that we need to talk."

"Yeah, we do. Is there any place private we can go?"

I thought about what would be open at this time of morning and would also give us at least a little privacy. "The mall?"

Not the most romantic spot, I thought, and then admonished myself. We didn't need romantic, we needed practical. The mall would be just fine. I gave him directions all the while wondering just how exactly Griffin's trip would play out. And I also wondered how many ways his sudden presence here would change not only my life, but Sadie's as well.

Our local mall had recently been renovated and an addition of a large outdoor entertainment area had been added. The outdoor area was considered fancy for our town and was dotted with small, pretty water fountains and several lounge areas which faced a huge flat screen TV that sat about 20 feet high on one outer wall. The lawn was used to host various classes from yoga to toddler's story time. And as I predicted, no one was there. We had the entire lawn to ourselves. I took off my shoes, enjoying the grass between my toes, and took a deep breath of early morning air. Any other day, I would have been enjoying a brisk walk around the neighborhood with Sadie at my side, riding along on her tricycle, but today clearly wasn't an average morning… at least not in my life.

I sat down on the grass and folded my legs under me.

Griffin sat down next to me. I shifted away from him, needing room for what I was about to say. I knew his nearness distracted me and I had too much to get off my chest to risk being distracted.

He cleared his throat and looked down at me. His dark brown eyes were studying me earnestly.

He reached out to touch my face and I pushed his hand away. He didn't seem surprised, but hurt nonetheless. He sighed. "Where should we start? I keep screwing this up, so why don't you start?"

I thought that was a brilliant idea. So, I led with a simple question: "Why are you here?"

"I messed up. Simple as that and I want the opportunity to make it up to you... and to our daughter."

"So, you want to be a part of her life?"

He nodded. "But I want more than that, I want both of you to be a part of my life."

"I'm not sure if that's such a good idea," I said, not looking away from him. In the past, I would have looked away, afraid to face him, but not today.

"If you give me a chance—"

"Why should I?"

"I know I can make you happy if you let me."

I frowned. "I'm not unhappy. And I hope you're not arrogant enough to think my happiness depends on you."

He rubbed at his face in frustration. "I'm screwing

this up big time." He reached for my hands and this time I let him hold them. I looked at him and realized this conversation was probably really hard for him, and I bet for the most part things usually came easy for him. I wasn't going to make this easy.

"I just want to be a part of your life and our daughter's life. You can decide what that entails. I'm not going to push you into doing something you'd rather not do. I'm not going to rush you to make a decision. I understand that right now you're probably not feeling that charitable towards me—"

"You got that right."

"But, I want to get to know her... and it would be a privilege if you'd allow me to do so."

"Nice speech," I said, pulling my hands away. "But flowery words that you probably thought up while on the plane ride here doesn't make up for the fact I've been mistreated by you and your family, specifically your mother."

He opened his mouth to interrupt and I held up my hand to silence him. "Let me say what I have to say."

He looked ready to argue again and I shot him a warning glance. "Let me say what I have to say or you can get back on a plane to L.A."

"Go ahead," he said reluctantly.

"I don't really want to focus on the past. What's done is done. You don't know your daughter. You haven't been around for the last four years of her life. You're a stranger to her. We're both to blame for that." I took a deep breath and continued, "But you have every right to be in her life and Sadie has every right to have a father."

"Sadie, that's her name? That's a beautiful name."

"It was my grandmother's name," I said, and doggedly continued, "We'll co-parent for Sadie's sake. While you're here, we can draw up a visitation schedule and custody agreement."

"That's not necessary. I'll agree to whatever you decide."

I gave him a long look. "I'm not sure I trust you."

"Nina—"

"I'm not finished." I took a deep breath, knowing that the next words out of my mouth would hurt not only him, but me. There was no way around it though, I would just push through the pain, because my next words needed to be said. I couldn't trust Griffin not to hurt me. His track record proved that. "For the sake of Sadie, I want everything to be civil between us, but you need to understand that there is no 'us'. Understood?"

He shook his head, "Why are you being like this?"

"Being like what?" I asked coldly.

"You know what I'm talking about... so cold and unfeeling. The other night you were writhing in my arms and now you want nothing to do with me? What's going on?"

"I'm tired. I'm tired of getting tossed aside by you and your family as if I'm not important, as if my feelings don't matter. I matter, Griffin, and until you realize that, there will be no us." I stood up then and said, "Take me home."

We rode back in silence. Griffin gripped the steering wheel tightly. You could tell that he was angry, but he didn't say a word. I'd surprised not only Griffin but myself earlier. I think what happened to my father had served to make me stronger. Just like having to raise Sadie alone had made me stronger, dealing with the aftermath of my dad's stroke had further developed my inner fortitude. No matter how much it hurt to tell Griffin that he wasn't welcome in my life, it had been necessary. I had to demand more if I wanted more. And what Griffin offered me wasn't enough. I was tired of hearing, "I'm sorry."

I know many women said they liked a guy who could admit when he was wrong. But I wanted more than that; I wanted someone who didn't have so many wrongs to apologize for. Griffin's apologies were like band-aids, but he and his family were the ones inflicting the pain. What good was covering a wound when one didn't have to be inflicted at all? That's how I felt about my relation-ship with Griffin. At least Griffin apologized for the harm his mother caused, but that wasn't enough. He needed to do better and I deserved better. I was done being hurt.

When he pulled up to my house, I said succinctly, "Meet us tomorrow at noon at the mall. Same spot."

He nodded, and then as an afterthought said, "Thank you."

I felt my resolve weakening, but I controlled it and resisted the urge to say something to ease the awkwardness between us. This was just how it had to be, I told myself as I walked away from his car and prepared myself for a conversation with my daughter about her father.

* * *

At exactly noon the next day, I waited for Griffin. He showed up with a bouquet made of candy and a giant teddy bear. He'd combed his hair straight back and was wearing a suit. He looked equal parts handsome and ridiculous.

"Did you really dress up to meet a four-year-old?"

He nodded and swallowed thickly, "I wanted to make a good impression."

"She's your daughter, not a potential business partner."

He looked down at his suit and then frowned.

"You're right... I don't know what the hell I was thinking."

"Watch your language around her."

"You're right. I'm just nervous." And I could tell he was. I peered at his forehead.

"Are you sweating, Griffin? She's a four-year-old, not a firing squad, it'll be fine."

He sat down heavily next to me and said, "Where is she?"

"She's skating with Kenny." I gestured to the ice skating rink that was open year round. It was conveniently located at the back of the mall near the lawn. "They should be on their way now."

I know I sounded calm and collected, but I was nervous too. I'd known this moment would come eventually, but I hadn't expected it to come now. It was too soon, wasn't it? Or maybe it was way overdue, depending on how you looked at it.

"Do you think she'll be afraid of me?" Griffin asked, breaking me away from my reverie. He was nervously picking at the imaginary lint on his pants. I tried to ignore how good he looked in his suit. And I ignored the fact that I was highly amused by his decision to wear a suit. He really was trying.

"I don't think so. She's pretty stranger-friendly. We're still working on that."

"Good. Not that being stranger-friendly is good, but

it's good that she won't be afraid of me. Do you think we should get her a bodyguard?"

"What?" I asked, my brows raised.

He shook his head, "Nothing." He switched gears, asking, "Does she know who I am?"

"She knows about you. I didn't keep you a secret. I've always mentioned you."

"Oh, thank you for that." He sounded surprised, but it was the truth. I answered any questions she had about her dad, but given that she was so young, luckily there hadn't been too many questions and my answers seemed to satisfy her.

I looked at him and saw the sincerity in his eyes. It made me uncomfortable. I was building a wall in my heart to protect myself from being hurt by him again, but those eyes of his were wreaking havoc on that plan.

I shrugged, trying to appear nonchalant. "I'm not a complete monster. I didn't lie to her and tell her that storks had dropped her off on my doorstep. I told her that she had a father out there who really loved her and one day she'd meet him. I just didn't think that day would be today."

"You really told her that?"

"Of course," I said softly. "I never stopped believing that maybe one day this would happen."

"I'm glad this is happening." He swallowed nervously and then said, "Do you think this is a good idea?"

I had to laugh. "I don't know, Griffin. Let's just go with it. Take it a day at a time and see how it goes."

That was my new motto. Dad had been released from the hospital and just like he was taking it one day at a time, I was determined to do the same. No pressure. At least, that's what I told myself.

I saw Kenny walking towards us. He was holding Sadie's hand and they were chatting about something. Then they started to skip together and I laughed as they approached.

"Kenny's really great with her."

"He's great with kids. He thought about being a teacher some time ago."

They came to a stop in front of us, laughing.

"Hi," Sadie said to Griffin immediately. "I saw you on my mommy's porch."

"Yes," he said softly, staring at her.

"You're very big," she said, and I laughed lightly.

"Yeah, he is pretty tall, isn't he?"

Kenny excused himself, saying, "I'll give you guys some time to get acquainted. I'll be at the food court if anyone needs me."

He quickly made himself scarce and we all watched him walk away as if hoping he would come back to make all of this less awkward.

"Sooo..." Griffin said, rocking back on his heels. "I'm your dad."

"Ok," Sadie said, "Mommy says you love me a whole lot. Like this much." She held her arms out wide.

Griffin smiled, finally starting to relax. "More like this much…" He stretched his arms out wide and Sadie's eyes lit up.

"Wow! That's a lot!"

She surprised us both then when she reached for his hand. "Come on, Daddy. Let's skate."

"I don't know how."

"I'll teach you. It's easy."

They walked away leaving me behind. I didn't know how I felt. Part of me wanted to cry. Well, all of me wanted to cry. I had to share my little girl and I wasn't used to it. But the other part of me wanted to cry because she'd taken to him instantly, as if he'd always been a part of her life. The guilt I felt over the years slowly faded. It felt like the huge burden was finally lifted from my shoulders.

I didn't know how we'd work it out since he lived in L.A. and we lived in Georgia, but for the sake of Sadie, I knew we'd find a way.

* * *

"Alright, Sadie. This is a hard one. Tell me when you're ready."

"I'm ready, Daddy!" she said excitedly. They were

sitting on my living room floor playing Trivia games that I told Griffin she was way too young to appreciate. Apparently, I'd been wrong.

"Ok, what is the capital of Florida? You have ten seconds to answer..." He started to count down, "10...9...8..."

She put her chin in her hand and looked thoughtful. "Tallapopsie!" she yelled and I couldn't help but giggle.

"Close, close," Griffin said. "Tallahassee... but Tallapopsie sounds so much better."

"Tallapopsie! Tallapopsie!" she sang as she bounced around the house in the tutu skirt Griffin had bought her. It was green with gold around the hem. It was the oddest looking tutu I'd ever seen and she loved it.

Nearly three months had passed since my father's stroke, and Griffin, to my surprise, had been around the whole time. He left every other weekend to attend to business, but always came back. He even showed up one weekend with Jackson and his wife. It had been a nice visit. Griffin had promised Sadie he'd bring back her cousin, Rory, when he went to California next time.

He talked about Rory so warmly that I wanted to meet her. I'd pretended not to notice that the only person who hadn't come out to meet Sadie was her grandmother, but I didn't dwell on it. Sadie was clearly loved and I wasn't going to let the absence of one person from her life make her feel otherwise.

The past three months hadn't been easy on any of my family, but Griffin had been a big help. I hadn't expected that. Kenny had returned to work a week after Dad's stroke, but he checked in on Dad all the time, so it was almost as if he had never left.

With Kenny gone and Mom busy taking care of Dad, I'd thought I would need to put Sadie in daycare during my peak working hours, but Griffin had stepped in and for the past three months he'd taken care of her. It had freed me up not only to get work done, but to also help Mom take Dad to his appointments.

I'd worried at first about how things would work out, but I needn't have worried at all. Sadie and Griffin were inseparable. She wouldn't eat dinner without Daddy. She wouldn't go to bed unless he tucked her in. She even insisted that he take her to preschool story time, which had been our activity. I had to admit, it had made me a little jealous.

As I'd asked, he had given me the space I wanted. He didn't ever talk about us as a couple. He only talked about us as parents. And I told myself that was fine. That was what I asked for, wasn't it? He was just honoring our agreement. Our agreement was that he could have a relationship with Sadie, but I was off limits.

But I would be lying if I said there weren't days where I wanted his attention, when I wanted him to disregard everything I said about us that day in the mall and just take me into his arms and hold me. I missed sex with him too, that was a given, but I could satisfy myself in that arena... all while thinking of him.

It was the other part, the emotional part, which was hard for me. Every time he smiled at Sadie, the wall I placed around my heart cracked a little. Each time he tucked her into bed or stopped her from tripping and falling into a wall—she was so clumsy—made me feel closer to him. And he treated me with the utmost respect. He never crossed any boundaries. It was as if the man who had followed me and practically stalked me around the set in California no longer existed. In his place was a family man who dedicated all his energy to making his little girl happy. And as a result, that little girl's mom was falling in love with that man.

I'd realized it early on and knew part of my hesitation about him being in her life was this exact scenario. I'd worried I wouldn't be satisfied with just him building a relationship with Sadie... that I would want a piece of him too... and I had been right. That's exactly what had happened.

Griffin had always occupied a space in my heart, but this new aspect of him, being a father, seemed to complete him. It seemed to make him a better man and it pulled at my heart.

I hid it well. I kept our conversations centered

around Sadie. I never let him catch me staring at him. I was doing well, but why did I feel so miserable?

Every Sunday we went to my parents' home for an early dinner and this time, I wanted to look nice. I wanted Griffin to notice me. I did my hair and put on a little makeup, hoping Griffin would notice. He arrived right on time and I instantly patted my hair and made sure my makeup looked alright.

My dad noticed and frowned. "Are you and the co-founder a thing now?" He still called Griffin Sadie's co-founder. He said he was still waiting for Griffin to "prove" himself, whatever that meant.

"What? No. What gave you that idea?"

"You're sprucing yourself up like you have a big date or something. You did the same thing whenever you'd go out with that geeky boy, what was his name? Brandon? Brent? Barry?"

I rolled my eyes, feeling like a teenager again. "Tim, Dad. His name was Tim."

"I was close..."

I shook my head. "You weren't even on the right letter."

He laughed and made his way to the table. He was walking and talking without an issue. Aside from the barely perceptible sloping of his eye, you couldn't tell that just three months ago he'd suffered a stroke. I knew that his hand on one side was still a problem sometimes, but it wasn't something that was outwardly noticeable.

While his back was turned, I snuck another look at my makeup and tried to appear nonchalant when Griffin came through the door with flowers for my mom, like he did every Sunday. He never gave me flowers, I thought to myself. He whispered something in my mom's ear and she laughed like an infatuated school girl.

"Aren't you guys chummy?" I said.

They both looked at each other in confusion and then back at me. "Don't be jealous, sweetheart. He hasn't ever been in the presence of such a beautiful woman before," she said.

I made a face at my mom and she laughed. "Fine, you want some attention. Griffin, tell my daughter how beautiful she looks."

I blushed. "That's not necessary."

He looked at me and let his gaze drift from my face to my neck, to my cleavage, to the rest of me. It felt like he spent minutes devouring me with his eyes, when in fact, it had only been a few seconds. He met my eyes and said, "Breathtaking as ever." He turned away from me. "Now, Mrs. Charles, what can I help you with?"

"Mrs. Charles was my mother-in-law, call me Ada... I insist."

Great, now they were on a first name basis, I thought

to myself, trying to forget the way Griffin's eyes had devoured me seconds ago.

We all sat down at the table and I felt self-conscious as I sat across from him, although it was always where I'd been seated since this dinner became our Sunday tradition.

"So, Griffin, how are you liking Georgia?"

"It's growing on me," he said, giving my dad an easy smile. "I used to go to Atlanta on business trips sometimes."

"Hotlanta is what I used to call it back in the day." I looked at my dad in surprise. He never called it Hotlanta.

Mom rolled her eyes at him. "Stop trying to sound cool."

"Trying? I am cool. Aren't I, Sadie?"

She nodded enthusiastically before taking a big bite out of a fried chicken wing.

"She has a great appetite... I wish I had her metabolism," my mom said looking sadly at the pudge that was starting around her middle.

"You're beautiful," Dad said, kissing her cheek.

Sadie giggled and said, "Kiss Mommy, Daddy!" I immediately froze but she kept cheering. "Kiss! Kiss! Kiss!"

"Oh, go ahead, don't disappoint the child," my mom

said helping herself to another round of mashed potatoes.

I smiled tightly at Griffin. He was looking at me wondering what to do, when Sadie said, "Get up, get up. Go kiss Mommy."

He got up slowly made his way around the table and kissed me gently on my cheek, just as my dad had done to my mom, and I pretended to be unaffected by it. It was over quickly, but the feel of his lips against my skin, his nearness, the light scent of his cologne were all going to be on my mind tonight, whether I liked it or not.

Thanksgiving arrived faster than I expected. We'd planned as a family to go visit my aunt's family in Orlando, Florida, but then Sadie came down with a cold that I soon caught, and Griffin wasn't scheduled to be back in town until later that day. Mom and Dad had wanted to cancel, but I knew Mom hadn't seen her sister in a while, so I wanted her to go.

"Don't worry about us," I said as she went to get back in the car after stopping by my house to kiss me and Sadie goodbye. I was feeling slightly better, just really tired from being sick so many days in a row.

"I feel so bad."

"Why?"

"It's the holidays... we should all be going as a family or not at all," she whined.

"Mom, you haven't seen Auntie Akila in two years. Go. Get out of here."

"Ada, get in the car," Dad said, leaning his head out the window. "I want to get there before the turkey's cold."

"I bet the turkey's still frozen," Mom said, "You know Akila, she always procrastinates."

"But she makes juicy turkey," Dad said.

"That's because she spends all her time doing nothing but going through recipes on Pinterest. I swear she's addicted—"

I missed the rest of her statement as she closed the door, tooted the horn, and then drove away.

That left just me, eventually Griffin, and Sadie around for Thanksgiving dinner and I hadn't prepared a thing. This Thanksgiving was an epic fail of historic proportions.

And I wasn't sure if Griffin was even going to stop by. He'd said he would, but then we'd all gotten sick and I hadn't heard from him since. He could still be on a plane for all I knew.

I walked back in to check on Sadie. She was still asleep. At the rate she was going, she would sleep through dinner, but honestly did it really matter? Thanksgiving was going to be non-existent this year.

Ten minutes after my parents pulled off, I spotted

Griffin's car in the distance. I waited for him on the front porch.

I felt bad. I knew he'd just gotten back from L.A. the night before. He must be exhausted, I thought to myself. Hungry and exhausted.

He pulled up and stepped out of the car. He'd grown a beard since moving here and it looked really good on him. It made him seem sort of like an upscale lumberjack, I thought with amusement.

He was dressed in jeans and a plain black t-shirt and he wore plain black and white sneakers. His wardrobe was a lot more casual than it had been in L.A., but I thought he looked just as attractive, if not more so.

I waved my hand hesitantly to say hello as he got out the car. He smiled at me and waved back. I was glad he was there. I didn't want to spend Thanksgiving alone.

I stuck my hands in the back pockets of my jeans and called out to him, "Just FYI—I have no food."

"I figured as much," he called back and began unloading stuff from the car. He placed two paper bags on the hood of his car and said, "I have dinner."

I cheered and gleefully bounded down the porch stairs to help.

"I saw your parents at the gate," he said as we carried the groceries in. My parents lived in a gated community, so it was no surprise he'd run into them. "They seemed excited about their trip to Orlando."

"They are, it's just too bad we all had to get infected with the plague."

"I'm feeling better now," he said.

"I still feel like crap."

"Well, you look good," he said glancing at me quickly and then looking away.

"Oh, thank you…" I hadn't expected the compliment. I was wearing a yellow tank top and a plain pair of skinny jeans. Nothing special. My hair was down because I'd at least brushed it today.

"You don't have to worry about cooking. I'll take care of our Thanksgiving feast."

"Really?"

"Yes, really. Why? You don't think I can pull it off."

"I wouldn't bet on it."

"Don't mess with a man on a mission," he said as he unpacked his groceries.

I watched him, checking out his backside once again. I couldn't help myself. He was crazy attractive in jeans. I watched the way his muscles pulled at the fabric of his shirt and noticed how broad his shoulders were. I wanted to walk up to him, wrap my arms around him, and lay my head on his back and just breathe in the scent of him.

He looked behind him suddenly and I pretended to be busy organizing the spice rack. He gave me a knowing look and I decided not to notice.

"Want to be useful and help out?"

"Not if I don't have to."

"Pretty please..."

"Well, since you're begging and all..."

I came over to help and noticed that none of the items he purchased could even remotely be considered Thanksgiving-ish.

It was a mixture of Italian ingredients and salad fixings.

"Not exactly Thanksgiving oriented," I commented

"Well, it was either Italian food and salad or eggs. Those are really the only things I know how to make."

"So, spaghetti or an omelet for Thanksgiving?" I tapped my chin and tried to look pensive as if it was a tough decision I had to make.

"Those are your choices, mademoiselle."

I smiled widely. "Spaghetti sounds delicious." It felt good to tease him again. It made me feel as if we were good friends, but I guess, over the months, that's exactly what we had become.

"How can I help?"

"You can help by taking a nap. You look exhausted."

He was right... I was exhausted.

"No, I want to help," I began to protest. He shook his head, nudged me towards the hallway and said, "Go take a nap. I'll wake you when everything's done."

I didn't bother to fight him. A nap sounded like a

godsend. He was right, rest was exactly what I needed. I walked to Sadie's room to check on her. I sat down on the bed next to her and stroked her hair as she slept, grateful that the worst was over and she was feeling better. I felt my eyelids growing heavy as I stroked her hair and within minutes I gave in to sleep, tucked next to my preschooler in a tiny twin size bed.

* * *

IT WAS pitch black in Sadie's room when I opened my eyes again. I'd been startled awake because I was floating in the air, a pair of strong arms carrying me, removing me from my awkward position on Sadie's bed.

I snuggled up against his chest thinking it was only a dream, but it clearly wasn't. His chest felt hard against my cheek and I could hear the steady beat of his heart near my ear.

"Where are you taking me?" I questioned drowsily.

"To your room. You were almost about to fall off the bed."

"Hmmm...." was all I said as I let my head fall back against his chest and I wrapped my arms around his neck. A girl could get used to this, I thought dreamily.

A minute later he was lowering me into my bed and then he walked quickly away. As he moved to close my door I sat up, "Griffin?"

"Yeah?" he said, pausing at my door.

"Can you come lie next to me? I mean, just for a little bit."

He paused. "You sure about that?" It was a loaded question, but I chose to pretend it wasn't. I couldn't see his expression in the shadows, but I knew what he was actually asking. And I knew without a doubt what my answer was.

"Yeah, I'm sure."

He came over slowly and slid his shoes off and he lay down next to me. We didn't touch, we just lay there in the dark next to each other.

"Did you have a good nap?" he asked, finally breaking the silence.

"Yeah, it was exactly what I needed. Did you finish cooking dinner?"

"Hours ago," he said.

"And Sadie didn't wake up at all?"

"She was up for a few minutes. She went to the bathroom and wanted some orange juice, but then went right back to bed."

"That cold kicked her butt. She's still exhausted. Poor thing."

"She'll be fine. She's a fighter like her mother."

I smiled and shifted a little closer to him, trying to see his face in the poorly lit room.

"Sorry, we slept through Thanksgiving..."

"No biggie."

He shifted a little in the bed as well and then brought his hand up to hold my own. We lay like that holding hands not saying a word. His face was only inches from my own and I could easily take a breath and breathe in the scent of him.

He slowly removed his hand from mine and brought it up to my face. He trailed the palm of his hand across my cheek, cupping it gently before letting go. He stroked my hair, lightly playing with the strands that randomly fell across my face and pushing the bangs that rested on my forehead away from my eyes. His hand was warm, and I sighed enjoying the feel of his soft touch. His touch was easy and familiar. And I realized how much I missed the easy intimacy between us.

I made the first move, leaning forward and gently resting my lips against his. He hesitated but he let me kiss him. I kept the kiss brief, not wanting to be greedy, but one wasn't enough. I had to kiss him again and this time there was no hesitation as his warm lips met my own. As the kiss became deeper, he took my hand again and held it. And we lay like that kissing each other, slowly, not rushing, as if we had all the time in the world to lie there and kiss our troubles away.

I finally pulled back and slowly sat up. I began to remove my clothes until I was completely naked.

"Are you sure about this?" he whispered, as I unzipped his pants, freeing his already erect penis.

"Yes," I said simply, before sliding his length into my mouth.

He moaned and thrust his hips up slowly, moving in and out of my mouth. With each of his movements, I sucked and licked the tip of his cock, using my hands to also pleasure him, stroking him up and down.

"Nina," he gasped, and I shushed him, not wanting to take the chance that we would wake Sadie.

I released him from my mouth and climbed on top of him, straddling his thighs. I placed my hands on his hard chest and slowly lowered myself onto his straining member. It was gradual because I was tight and he was bigger than I remembered. He felt amazing as my wet lips fully enveloped him, growing wetter as he filled me, inch by glorious inch.

And when he was fully inside, I began to rock my hips, riding him slowly at first before picking up the pace as he stroked my back, my arms, my neck, and hair.

His soft touches electrified my body. Everywhere he touched me was like an erogenous zone and I found myself coming, taking him with me as the pleasure became too much to bear and my whole body shook, trying to adjust to the waves of pleasure that overtook it. I collapsed against his chest, gasping his name.

He came then, bucking into me, pressing my hips

down, pushing even deeper into me than before and then I felt his warmth spill into me as he quietly whispered my name.

I didn't want to get off him, but I wanted him to be comfortable.

I went to crawl off, when he said, "No, stay. Just let me hold you."

I didn't protest. Instead I stayed right there... resting with him still buried deep inside me. He continued to stroke my back and I don't know how long it was before I drifted off. I only knew that I was still wet when I woke again, and he was stiffening inside me.

We made love again slowly, not rushing. Afterward, I fell asleep one last time on top of him, nestled against his chest.

The sun peaking in through the blinds woke me up and I slowly slid Griffin out of me. I realized that we'd spent the whole night connected and not just physically.

I immediately missed the way he filled me and apparently, he missed it too. He promptly wrapped his arms around me and pulled me close.

"We have to get up," I said softly as he buried his head in the crook of my neck and started to nuzzle me.

I gasped. "Griffin, don't start..."

"But you smell so good, so sweet. And your skin... it's so smooth." He continued to nuzzle my neck and I curled my body around his, loving the feel of him.

I could feel him hardening against my thigh and couldn't help rubbing against it as I brought his face to mine and kissed him warmly on the mouth.

"Good morning to you too, Griffin."

He gave me a big smile and then said, "Do I have morning breath?"

I giggled, "I'm pretending not to notice."

He surprised me by sitting up abruptly and turning me so that I was now sitting up in his lap. He wrapped his arms around me and kissed me briefly on the lips.

"I know I spent the night inside of you, but the part I enjoyed the most was just holding you." I looked into his brown eyes and knew he meant every word of it. "I missed holding you so much."

"I missed being in your arms," I said wanting him to know the truth. "I missed being with you."

"Why didn't you say something sooner?" he asked.

"I just wanted to know, to be sure that you respected me, that you took me seriously. That you cared about me."

He shook his head as if he didn't understand me. "Don't ever doubt that I respect and care about you. Our time together has been colored by a series of mistakes on my part, I know that now. But I want you to understand I never only wanted your body. Yes, you've always been a great lover... but you're also caring, and quirky, and smart. You're a great daughter, friend and mother.

You made me a better man, Nina, and overall just a better person. Knowing you has made me better. I owe my happiness to you."

Tears clouded my eyes and I wiped them away. His words moved me, as if they had touched my soul.

He brushed my tears away with small kisses under my eyes. I felt self-conscious and vulnerable all of a sudden, but I wasn't sure why.

"Don't shy away from me," he said as he turned my face to his and looked me straight in the eyes. "You're a wonderful person and everyone loves you. It's impossible not to love you. And I love you."

I didn't know what to say. I was speechless. And so, I said the only thing that came to mind, "Happy Thanksgiving."

"That was yesterday," he said.

"Ok then, how about this? I love you too, Grant 'Griffin' Wallace."

He laughed and brought my head down to his for another long, blissful kiss.

# EPILOGUE

I stood on the balcony overlooking the lake below us. It was beautiful, a rich dark blue and surrounded by tall wildflowers. The pier that led to the lake was covered in flowers as well, ending right at the edge of the pier where Griffin and I were to be married.

I wasn't nervous. All I felt was happiness. Griffin was everything that I wanted in a man. And finally, we'd be together.

I was so lost in thought that I didn't hear when someone opened the door. It was my mom and she gave me a smile.

"You look beautiful! Gosh, I'm so jealous. Your dad and I got married at the courthouse the next county over. It wasn't exactly a great photo moment. I had all sorts of questionable fluids on my scrubs."

I'd heard that story many times before and it was always amusing. She and Dad had gotten married during her lunch break, right after she'd helped deliver triplets on the emergency room floor.

"But you, you look so perfect. So beautiful. I would call you angelic if I didn't know any better," she teased, making me smile. "So, are you ready?"

I nodded. "Definitely. Is Dad ready?"

"He's waiting downstairs for you. The stairs are still a little hard for him."

Excitedly, I made my way downstairs where Dad was sitting patiently for me in a white linen suit.

"Don't you look sharp today!" said Dad, standing up gingerly. He was using a cane, not because he needed it but because he wanted to make a fashion statement. My dad was too much sometimes, but it did make him look quite debonair. I made a mental note to tell him that later.

"Thanks, Dad," I said. I was amused by his compliment. Who used the word "sharp" to describe their daughter in a wedding dress? My dad did.

"Shall we?" he asked, with a teasing smile on his face. I think he might have been more excited about making a grand appearance than I was.

"Let's do this." I hooked my arm through the one he offered and my mom gave us a big smile before she disappeared outside.

Suddenly, I started to feel a little nervous as the music began. As if sensing it, Dad reached up and patted my hand. "It's alright to be nervous, little one."

"I didn't expect this."

"It'll pass."

"I hope I don't trip over my train."

He said, "If you do, I'll trip too, that way no one will pay attention to you. They'll be too busy trying to help up the geriatric case."

"Great plan, Dad."

He chuckled.

I couldn't help myself as I peeked around the corner to catch a glimpse of my daughter as she walked down the pier.

Sadie looked adorable as a flower girl. She was dressed in a yellow poufy dress and had a crown of flowers in her hair. She was the perfect flower girl, I thought to myself, as she tossed flowers down the pier in wild abandon. A few people had to dodge flowers that smacked them in the face. I made a mental note to get Sadie into t-ball.

And then when she made it to the front, Griffin picked her up and placed a kiss on her forehead. She made a face and he laughed. She went to go stand next to her cousin Rory who was also a member of the wedding party. They held hands while holding their baskets and smiled big, mischievous smiles at each other. I knew Nora, Rory's mother, wasn't coming to the wedding, but I hoped one day, when she got better, that I'd be able to meet her.

The music changed, signaling that it was finally my turn to make an entrance. Dad and I turned the corner and started our journey down the pier. My nervousness instantly disappeared. I looked towards my cousin Kenny who was my best man. He beamed at me and I smiled back. I knew Cyril was somewhere in the crowd. I found him easily given he was the only guest wearing a cowboy hat. He'd stuck to his plans and bought the winery in Texas and to my surprise, Kenny had decided to join him after all. And as luck would have it, they were having a great time. They were making new friends and learning a lot about the wine business. It all seemed to be working out.

But life was full of surprises. Griffin had relocated his headquarters to Georgia, but had kept his apartment in L.A. so that we would always have a place to call home whenever we went to California to visit.

The only person who'd been upset by the move was Griffin's now best man Jackson, who didn't like the idea of having his big brother permanently more than half way across the country. Speaking of Jackson, he was up to his usual silliness as he stood across from Kenny giving me a thumbs up as my father and I slowly made our way in their direction.

Jackson suddenly caught the eyes of someone in the crowd and dropped his hands instantly. I could tell without looking who that someone was.... my future mother-in-law.

I passed by Mrs. Wallace who sat next to my mother. We were civil towards each other, but I sincerely doubted I would ever be calling her "Mom". It didn't matter though, she was building a relationship with Sadie and I would do anything for Sadie, even if that meant putting up with Christmas dinners with Loretta, which is what she now insisted I call her. She had warmed a little towards me when she realized I hadn't spent $250,000 dollars on shoes and purses. I'd put it all in a trust fund for Sadie when she'd been about a year old.

And then I raised my eyes and looked at the man who watched me as if I were the only person in the world.

He looked gorgeous. He'd trimmed his beard and had grown his hair out a little. I liked his new look. It suited him. I liked to think of him as my corporate lumberjack.

What felt like seconds later, my dad was kissing my cheek and handing me off to him.

I looked up at my future husband and smiled. He smiled back at me and whispered in my ear, "Thanks for showing up."

"Thanks for inviting me," I whispered back.

As I stood looking at him, I knew I'd made the right choice. Our day had finally come and we would be united forever.

The officiant cleared his throat to get our attention and we promised forever to each other in front of all our family and friends. Before I knew it, the ceremony was over and Griffin and I leaned towards each other and sealed our vows with a kiss.

The crowd clapped and cheered. Mrs. Wallace, of course, clapped a few times and looked around for something more interesting to do.

We walked through the crowd of well-wishers, hand-in-hand. Somehow, Sadie had made her way to the beginning of the pier and started throwing rice at us, a bit too hard. I was starting to change my mind about signing her up for t-ball.

I stood next to the car where Griffin's driver, Geoff, was waiting to drive us to the reception.

I knew I was supposed to wait until the reception to throw the bouquet, but in my excitement, I threw it then instead. I turned around and tossed it straight over my head. I turned just in time to watch it fly through the air and it landed with a smack in Mrs. Wallace's hands. I shrugged my shoulders and laughed. She looked horrified. I thought terror was a good look on her.

"See you at the reception!" Sadie yelled to us, already racing to the car that would escort the wedding party to the other building where the reception was to be held. My dad and mom raced behind her, barely keeping up. Griffin and I concealed our laughter, but watching my parents chase down their energetic granddaughter was quite a sight to behold.

Once we knew she was safe, Griffin held the door open for me as I slid into the car. He then slid in next to me with a wide grin on his face. "Now that was a good time, don't you think, Mrs. Wallace?"

"Mrs. Wallace is my mother-in-law, call me Nina," I said jokingly.

He leaned forward and kissed me. He then leaned down and placed his head against my belly. "Hey, little buddy, are you ready for some wedding cake?"

I felt a little flutter in my belly and smiled up at Griffin. "I felt a kick, so I'm going to go with yes." We were expecting our second child in a little less than four months. He had been a surprise... a very welcome surprise.

"I love you, Nina."

"And I love you, Griffin. Or should I call you Grant?"

"Don't you dare."

I gave him a mischievous smile. "I feel like there's a story behind that nickname of yours..."

"I'll tell you another time… Right now, I just want to kiss my wife."

And so, he did.

**DARK DESIRES**
~ A billionaire dark romance series ~
Dark Desire
Dark Rules
Dark Secret
Dark Time
Dark Truth

**BARRE TO BAR**
~ A billionaire second chance series ~
Dancing With Lies
Dancing With Temptation
Dancing With Doubt
Dancing With Guilt
Dancing With Redemption

**TWISTED INTENTION**
~ A billionaire revenge romance series ~
Twisted Beauty
Twisted Love
Twisted Fate


**Mafia's Obsession**
~ A hot mafia romance series ~
Mafia's Dirty Secret
Mafia's Fake Bride
Mafia's Final Play


**Screaming Demons**
~ An MC romance series full of suspense ~
Rough Start
Rough Ride
Rough Choice
Rough Patch
Rough Return
Rough Road
Rough Trip
Rough Night
Rough Love


**Standalone Contemporary Romance**
Billionaire in Vegas
Billionaire Hunt

Billionaire's Game
Billionaire Retreat
Billionaire On Air
A Chance To Love
Somebody To Love
Not Mine To Love


Check out Summer's entire collection at
**www.summercooper.com/books**

# ABOUT SUMMER COOPER

Thank you so much for reading. Without you, it wouldn't be possible for me to be a full-time author. I hope you enjoy reading my books as much as I do writing them.

Besides (obviously!) reading and writing, I also love cuddling my dogs, shouting at Alexa, being upside down (aka Yoga) and driving my family cray-cray!

Get in touch at
hello@summercooper.com
www.summercooper.com

facebook.com/summercooperauthor
instagram.com/summercooperauthor
goodreads.com/summercooper
bookbub.com/profile/summer-cooper

www.ingramcontent.com/pod-product-compliance
Lightning Source LLC
Chambersburg PA
CBHW051306210726
48287CB00002B/694